Johannes

A 'Madeline's Secret' Companion Book

Wendy

You're a cut above
everybody else !!

June 2019

Written by
Kevin Weisbeck

Kevin Weisbeck

Johannes

An Owlstone Book

Published as a Print-on-Demand book
through the Amazon Company,
for the author Kevin Weisbeck.

Printed in the United States of America
This is a work of fiction. Names, characters, and incidents
either are the product of the author's imagination or are used
fictitiously. Any resemblance to actual persons, living or
dead, or events is entirely coincidental.

Cover design by Kevin Weisbeck and Dan Huckle
Danhuckle.com
Special Thanks to Vincent Van Gogh
Cover - Café Terrace at Night

First printing, May 2019

Kevin Weisbeck

Johannes

Dedication

A special thanks to Sherry and all the members of the *Write Away* writer's group. Your endless hours of listening not only helped me to believe, but has pushed me further than I ever thought possible.

Thank you Morgan and Franklyn, two cats that have kept me company throughout it all…not that I listen to their writing tips.

And let's not forget Frankfurt and Paris. Your culture is inspiring, the food is amazing, and your beer (Frankfurt) is well worth the price of a plane ticket. Not to worry France, you still have wine.

Chapter one

My parent's favourite church stood as proud as a statue amongst the smaller houses, albeit stained by the many years of war and death. It was a modest building, with only a dozen pews. I took my place on the right side, up at the front. Six stained glass windows cast colours throughout the room, putting a smile on my face. The kaleidoscope of light took the edge off of why we were all here. It was a welcome distraction.

Up on the stage, behind an aged oak altar, Mrs. Browning brought the pipe organ to life. Above her, a larger-than-life Crucifix hung on the back wall. To most, it was a reminder of where we'd all come from, if you believed. Today I wasn't sure I was a believer, because in the open space in front of the altar, two recently sealed coffins had filled my heart with doubt.

Over my shoulder I could see that seating was scarce. Most people were standing along the sides. Why was I surprised, with my parents being loved by so many? Other than that time when Dad heckled that Oompah band off the stage in Römer Square, they were the perfect neighbours, the perfect churchgoers, and the perfect friends to half of Frankfurt. In Dad's defence, he'd had a lot to drink that day, and that band was embarrassingly bad.

Hannah, Danny Friedrich's wife, was staring at me when I looked her way. She'd been crying and quickly motioned with her hand for me to call her. I imagined her being thrust into a therapeutic baking spree after finding out about my parent's death. It was what women like her did. I forced a smile and nodded. She was Mom's favourite bridge partner.

I slowly panned the room to see that quite a few eyes were being dabbed by handkerchiefs. Damn, these were good people. At the door more cousins and friends were trying to make their way into the church. I should have had the ceremony at St. Catherine's. It was bigger. But Mom and Dad loved St. Joseph's. It was their church, their friend's church. I just hope the walls don't fail us. We'd spill into the streets like candy bursting from a piñata.

One of the ushers made his way to the altar. "Please be seated. If you cannot find a seat, then please remain where you are. We're about to start."

I sat back as people shuffled into spots behind me and my eyes never left the priest as he entered from the left. He was dangling a censer from a chain. It wafted an aromatic smoke as he walked around my mother's coffin first and then my father's. It smelled nice and placed a fog in my brain. In that fog I was walking along the Seine with Rebecca. As usual, she was talking and I was listening. She had such a beautiful tone in her voice.

She'd been telling me about a wallpaper she'd found. If I remember right, it had flowers and she wanted it for the bathroom. I needed to put my foot down and I did. A man can put up with many things, but pansies where he pees? I think not. It was the last time we'd talked.

The Priest made his way up to the altar and started mass by reciting the twenty-third Psalm. Mom loved that one. I did too. A hand landed softly on my shoulder, but I didn't bother to turn around to see whom it belonged to. Instead I shut it all out and let myself dip back into the fog.

Shortly after Rebecca and I had discussed the mismatch of flowers and toilets, she was off to see her sister, Madeline. I was off to the pub where I got the call from my aunt that my parent's car had slipped off the road and into the Rhine River. They were driving back from Rüdesheim. They couldn't tell me if they were okay or not, but everyone was heading to the hospital.

Johannes

There was a flight leaving for Frankfurt an hour later and I'd be on it. Marcus, my best friend, was with me and drove me out to the airport. I didn't even have a suitcase with me. When I landed, my Uncle was waiting. He took me over to the hospital only to find out that I had lost them both.

My aunt, God love her soul, had badgered the doctors to tidy up the bodies so that I wouldn't be horrified when I saw them. I'd have to identify them, protocol and all. They looked calm, lifeless. I still regret kissing my mother on the cheek. Her skin was so cold, making everything so real.

The Priest broke my fog again as he rattled off a few words of praise and then asked us all to rise. We did, and he started one of the hymns. I can't remember which one it was, nor did I join in because back at that hospital I was identifying my parents, signing off on the police report, and making a call to Rebecca. I'd left without saying goodbye, but I knew she'd understand. She was as much about family as I was. I had expected her to be home, but was surprised when her father answered. When I asked if Rebecca was there he broke into an open sob.

It turned out he had a key to our place and had let himself in. He was willing to stay there until I got home, all night, if that was what it took. He wanted to be with me when he told me about the car accident involving Rebecca, Madeline and her son Nicolas.

That same freak snowstorm that had devastated central Germany had also pushed its way through parts of France. Paris was hit with three inches and it had snarled traffic everywhere. It had also caused a moving van to slide through a stop sign and strike the very car that Rebecca was in. While her sister Madeline and nephew Nicolas were okay, the accident had ended the life of my Rebecca.

Hearing that, I had dropped to my knees, told him how sorry I was and politely hung up before puking all over the carpet. Days later, I can still taste that vile shit in my mouth. I need a drink.

The Priest had us sitting again as he read a few verses from the bible. The hand from before lands back on my shoulder. It's bad enough that I've lost not only my parents and the woman I love, but I have to sit here amongst all these people and listen to this Priest's endless sermon. Trust me, I want to believe. It's just that I'd rather be anywhere else and nursing a cold beer.

I looked over my shoulder at the doors, wondering if anybody would miss me if I ducked out. That was when I saw them sitting directly behind me. I noticed Fast Eddy Cruiser first. He was staring at the stained glass much like a cat might stare at a bird on the bottom branch of a tree. The hand on my shoulder belonged to a long lost friend named Heidi. She passed me a smile like we'd just gone to a movie and shared a couple hours of laughs and a bag of popcorn.

I hadn't seen either of them in ten years and, as nice as it was to look into those dark brown eyes of hers again, it sent a shiver up my spine.

Chapter two

Back at my parent's house the first wave of relatives were making their way up the sidewalk. The men carried bottles of wine, whiskey and beer while the women carried casserole dishes. I have no idea what I'll do with so much food. I sure hope my friends, Ingrid and Marcus, like leftovers.

I put the food on the table with the sliced meats, cheeses and buns that I'd bought earlier. I also found a few boxes of frozen cookies and squares in the freezer. Mom had been busy. There was a greedy part of me that wanted to leave them in the freezer. She always baked with such love. It was all I had left of her cooking.

Ingrid came up behind me with a coffee and a cookie. The brew smelled more like Irish Cream than coffee. "How you holding up?"

"Enjoy that cookie. Mom made it."

"I know she did. You can't get cookies like this at the patisserie."

"Where's Marcus?"

"He had to stop by the office, work stuff."

"Really?"

"No. He's a little messed up over this. Don't get me wrong, I love the guy, but he sucks when it comes to anything emotional. He wants to talk to you about everything, yet he knows it will upset you. That's the last thing he wants to do."

"I'm okay to talk. You can tell him that."

"I already told him. He just wants everything to be okay."

"Not much he can do about this."

"He needs time to figure that out." Ingrid gave me a hug and a kiss on the cheek. "Me, I'm the smart one. I know that all I can do is be here with you and eat your mother's delicious cookies. I've also got an imported bottle of Vodka, the good stuff, for when you want to talk, cry, and rant. I don't judge. I just drink my share."

I held her close and whispered, "Thank you for being you."

When she stepped back her eyes were damp. "I'm sorry about Rebecca. She was a pretty special girl."

"I know."

Ingrid batted her eyes to push back the tears, shot me a sympathetic wink and started for the living room. She'd become a good friend to me and an even better one to Rebecca. I knew she was hurting. Me, I'd found a well-needed numbness.

Since I was still in control, and Peter Krandle was looking at me the way a pimply-faced teenager looked at a girl at a school dance, I figured I'd go over and say hello. He was my father's lawyer and a friend of the family since I was a kid. He wasn't the invited-for-Christmas kind of friend, but we often ran into him and his wife at birthday parties, milestone anniversaries and... funerals.

I held out my hand. "Hello, Mr Krandle. So nice of you to come."

He took my hand and shook it. "I'm so sorry for your loss, Jon. I still have a hard time believing they're..."

"I know." I slipped my hands into the front pockets of my pants. "I got the envelope from your office yesterday, but I haven't looked at it yet. I, uh..."

"I'm sorry. I know it hasn't been that easy, but we need to go over a few things."

"I'll look at it tonight after everybody leaves."

"I've got a better idea. Drop by the office tomorrow and bring the envelope. I can explain everything and we can get the details sorted out. Some of it is time sensitive."

"Yes, we can do that. I'm not really good with the legal stuff."

"Neither was your dad." He smiled a crooked smile and placed a hand on my shoulder. "See you tomorrow around ten?"

"Okay. Ten works. Thanks, Mr Krandle."

Still numb, I never felt his hand lift off my shoulder. He walked away while I stared off at the people in the room. I put on my happy face for them. They were hurting and I was hurting. There was no reason to dwell on it. What I needed was one of my mother's butter tarts.

Marcus met me at the table. "Hey, Jon."

"You made it." I tried not to sound surprised.

"This is hard. It's one thing to lose your parents. It's bullshit to lose Rebecca too."

"I agree." I grabbed a butter tart. "You know we don't need to talk about any of this. I know how you feel."

"We don't?"

"No, Marcus. Girls talk about feelings and live to analyse moments like this. Guys go out, tip a few beers back and maybe end up fighting strangers in the back alley. You want to help me out, buy me a beer after I meet with my lawyer tomorrow."

"I can do that."

His eyes wandered as he finished that sentence. My eyes followed his until I saw what he saw. It was Fast Eddy and Heidi.

"What the hell are they doing here?" he asked.

I shrugged. "They were at the church earlier too. When was the last time we saw them?"

"I think it was in our past life." He couldn't take his eyes off of them. "Did they say anything?"

"No, and I didn't ask. I mean, I haven't even thought about them in years. I thought we were free of them. How do you think they found us?"

"You can ask them. They're coming over."

Heidi walked ahead of Eddie and spoke first. "Long time no see. How you guys been doing?"

Marcus didn't hesitate. "What do you want?"

"Nothing. I mean I wanted to give Johannes my regards." She was biting her lip as she turned to me. "This is such a sad day for you. I'm sorry."

"Thanks, Heidi. Don't let Marcus throw you. We are glad to see you guys. It's just been such a long time, and the last time we talked, it was pretty intense."

"Oh, I get it. I never thought I'd ever see you two again."

Marcus didn't let up. "How'd you find us?"

"Total fluke. We were in Frankfurt on business. I'm a real estate agent and Eddie is a regular handyman. I have a bit of savings and was looking for a fixer-upper as an investment property."

"So?"

"Oh, I was reading the paper over morning coffee yesterday when I read about your parent's funeral. I couldn't miss it."

Marcus nodded. "Okay. How'd you know to come here?"

"Your neighbour was at the funeral. He gave me the address when I told him we were friends from way back."

Chapter three

Dishes rattling in the sink woke me from a slumber that could have lasted the rest of my life, if I had let it. It didn't and walked into the kitchen where I found Ingrid elbow deep in soapy suds and dirty plates.

"What the hell are you doing here? Don't you sleep?"

"Morning sunshine. It's nine o'clock. The day is half over."

"Nine? In the morning?" I tried to blink away the sleep. "Is Marcus here?"

"Who do you think was outside cutting the grass?"

"What? I have neighbours. You can't be cutting the grass this early."

"We waited until we heard other lawnmowers. Then it was fair game. Besides, these are your parent's neighbours. They'd never be upset."

I had to agree. These people oozed goodness. Half of them were here last night eating Mom's baking, drinking Dad's scotch. "So how are you doing?"

She finished washing the plate she was holding, rinsed it and put it in the rack. She didn't turn around. "I'll be okay. I just have to figure out why."

"Good luck." I picked up a towel and started drying.

"I think this is the last of them." Marcus entered the room with a couple of cups and a handful of cutlery. "Oh look, Sleeping Beauty is up. You feeling okay?"

The head was a little rough. Heidi had started in on Dad's Galliano and Schnapps, pouring me one after another. It seemed like a good idea at the time. "Why'd you let me drink that shit?"

Ingrid took the dishes from Marcus. "We didn't know you needed a babysitter. Besides, it was the first time we'd heard you laugh all week."

"I was laughing?"

"We all were. Eddy still has a way with storytelling. When he told that one about the old lady wearing the PI t-shirt and pushing the baby buggy full of chickens, I almost peed myself."

"The Pecker Inspector." I started to laugh. "That is a good one. How long did they stay?"

"They left shortly after midnight," Marcus answered. "When they left the rest followed. They were the life of the party."

Except it wasn't a party. It was a wake. Fast Eddy Cruiser always had a way of making the best of a crappy situation. It was his nature. The man couldn't stand anything being serious. "Did anybody ask why they were here, other than the lame real estate story?"

Ingrid pulled the rubber gloves off and set them on the edge of the sink. "I'm going to do some digging. Not sure why they're here but you can be sure it's not good."

"I agree." I looked around. The house was as tidy as if my mother had done it herself. "Thanks guys. Hey, can I get one more favour?"

"Ask away," Marcus offered.

"I've got a lawyer appointment with Mr Krandle. Think I could bum a ride?"

Ingrid moved beside Marcus and let him put his hand around her waist. "We'll do one better. We'll go with you and then take you out for lunch. First I need a favour from you. Phone Rebecca's family."

I watched the arm slip around her. "What's going on here? Are you two…?"

"Don't change the subject and do not make a big deal about this," Ingrid scolded. "We've known each other for some time now and I don't know if it was Rebecca's constant badgering me to act on my feelings or what, but last night I made a move."

"You made a move?" Marcus chuffed. "I thought I made the move."

"You're right. You made the move." She rolled her eyes. "Regardless, we're gonna give this romance thing a try. You need to phone them."

"I know. I'll do it when we get back." I started for the bedroom to change. "I'll only be a minute."

I actually took four minutes. I needed to find one of Dad's shirts. I still didn't have any nice clothes. Ingrid and Marcus had packed toiletries and casual outfits. Good thing Dad had a lot of dress shirts and suit pants.

Marcus drove and got us to the office with minutes to spare. When I walked in Mr Krandle was standing by his secretary's desk.

"Come in, Jon."

The three of us stepped into his office and sat in the chairs across from him. Mr Krandle opened the envelope and spread the papers out. "I need three signatures. The one on this set of papers allows you to have everything that belonged to your parents. It's a Will of sorts. I can have everything transferred into your name in about three days. I just have to run this before a judge for his signature. It's pretty standard."

He let me sign it and shuffled another set of papers before me. "This one allows me to take my fees from your parent's bank account."

I signed it and looked over at the third set of papers. Mr Krandle was guarding those ones. "And those?"

"Maybe we could go over these ones alone." He gave Ingrid and Marcus uncertain glances. "These are a little more personal."

"These are my best friends. They're good."

"If you're sure."

"I am." The papers were slid in front of me and I started reading. I wasn't sure what I was looking at first. I needed clarity. "What is this?"

Before your mother met your father she was seeing somebody. The man was abusive and she left him. Your father came along and swept her off her feet."

"Did you know them at the time?"

11

"I knew your father." He continued. "Four months into their courtship she realised she was pregnant. It wasn't your father's doing. Your Dad wasn't happy about this, but he loved her enough to want her in his life."

I felt the blood draining from my face. "So he wasn't my father?"

"No. He was definitely your father. This pregnancy happened before you were born. Your parents were already married."

"So what happened?"

"Your mother was adamant about having this child. It wasn't the baby's fault his father was abusive. Your Dad however couldn't allow this child into their lives, so after she gave birth, the child was given up for adoption."

I sat back and tried to let this register. Mom was pregnant and had a child. She gave it up to be with Dad. This child was nothing to Dad, but it was her baby. That made it a sibling to me. "Boy or a girl?"

"It was a boy."

Chapter four

As much as I wanted to, I couldn't ask Marcus and Ingrid to stay in Germany. They wanted to and had even offered to push their flight to tomorrow, but I knew they had work to do. The big concern for them, was I okay? Hell, I was more than okay. Mixed feelings swirled inside my head like the leaves in an autumn windstorm. I'd lost my parents and the woman I loved. I was alone and yet I'd been given a breath of life. I was given a brother.

I'd been quiet earlier while Marcus drove us back from the lawyer's office. It was a time to process. Now that they were on their way back to Germany, I wanted to talk. I wanted to start looking for him. I'd do that tomorrow.

First, there was something I'd promised Ingrid. I picked up the phone. I held it in my hand and stared at it. What would I tell them? Today they put their daughter in the same cold ground that I'd put my parents in. They'd shed tears and listened as kind words smothered them like an unwanted blanket. Anything I say would surely be lumped into that same unwanted weave of sympathy and sorrow. I dropped the phone back into its cradle and went to the fridge for a beer.

It went down like water and a second was a must. I didn't want it on an empty stomach so I heated up some leftover cabbage roll casserole in the microwave. My parents had a microwave. It was probably the only thing they had bought in the last twenty years. There was no computer, no gas fireplace or even an answering machine, yet they went out and bought a damn microwave. Go figure. I bet it was more for Dad. Mom never would have used it when there was a perfectly good oven in the house.

I was ready to grab a second bowl of food when there was a knock on the door. My first thought was that Marcus had missed his flight. I half expected them to be standing there when I opened the door. Instead, Heidi was standing there, looking a little lost like a vacuum sales person on their first day.

"Can I come in, Jon?"

"Sure. Where's the Cruiser?"

"You know he hates it when you call him that."

"I know." I stepped aside to let her in. "Are you hungry?"

She stepped halfway through the doorway and turned to give me a hug. "Damn I missed you."

I hugged her back. There was a part of me that had always wondered how she was doing. It had been a decade and I was sure there were stories to tell. She looked good, but I had to believe it had been hard. The way we said good bye, the reasons we had to go our separate ways, it wasn't fair. But if there was anything I'd learned about life lately, it was that nothing was fair and there were no guarantees. "I've missed you too."

She let go and stepped inside. "Do you mean that?"

"You know better than to ask that." I closed the door.

Heidi turned back to me as if we were still dating. Her gaze was an obvious one. Was I seeing somebody? She wanted to ask me, but couldn't force the words out. Instead she put her hands on my arms and moved in closer. Should she kiss me? Could she get away with it? Her eyes danced around looking for any kind of sign.

She was once a lover and an even better friend. We had dated and dedicated ourselves to looking out for each other. She deserved to know. "I not only lost my parents, but I was seeing this girl back in Paris. We were engaged. She died in the same snowstorm when it hit there. She was also in a car accident."

Heidi's lustful stare wilted into an honest sorrow as she struggled to keep her jaw from dropping to the floor. "I am so sorry, Jon. I had no idea. If you want, I can go. God, I feel like such an idiot now."

"You didn't know." I let her pull away. "You never told me if you were hungry or not."

She laughed. "You always had a way with forgiving my stupidity. It's like you understood I was cursed with bad judgement and even worst timing. Again, I'm sorry, and yes, if you're offering, I'm starving."

"Step into the kitchen. I'll dish you up a bowl. Wanna beer?"

"Hell ya." She shook her long auburn locks, trying to shake the last of the embarrassment.

"I don't think you ever told me why you were here."

"Uh, real estate. You losing your memory in your old age?"

"Oh, I remember that story, just like I remember the one about the old lady and the chickens. Now why are you really here?"

"You're an ass."

"And yet you sit here in my kitchen eating my food and drinking my beer."

""No doubt. Good thing you're cute or I'd be out of here."

"Seriously, why are you here?"

"I love you, Jon. And for that reason I'm not going to tell you."

"What are you and Fast Eddy up to?"

"It is better you don't know, and no, I'm not doing anything illegal. I gave that up when we all decided to fly straight. I'm still flying straight, Jon."

"You sure?"

"You worry too much." She took a swig from her beer. "What have you been up to?"

"I do contract work, carpentry, electrical. It's been pretty good to me. What about you?"

"I went to school and became a teacher. I get to turn unruly imps into budding young intellectuals. It's been a lot of fun."

"I gotta say, I'm surprised."

"I know, right? Who'd of thought me of all people would become a teacher. When I think of all the things I put my teachers through."

"Like that time you organised the bra burning."

"Oh gee, fifty or more girls topless around a campfire. I'll bet that was a pretty good day for you boys."

"You were all ten and eleven. It was more a giggle fest where you girls showed off your mosquito bites. I think it was more memorable to you, than us."

"Bullshit. We saw you guys staring."

I moved us to the living room and took a spot on the couch. "Sorry. Dad's television only picks up news channels. I don't think he splurged for cable."

"That's okay. I miss talking to you." She took a spot on the other end of the couch and spun to face me. Cross-legged, she leaned against the throw pillow and armrest. "Is it okay to talk like we used to?"

"Definitely."

"Means I might stuff my foot in my mouth. You know I'm good for doing that."

"I've always enjoyed watching you do that."

"Okay, so what now? I mean you've lost your parents and your girlfriend. That's a pretty big hit."

"Wow. That's uh, pretty blunt, even for you."

"I know, but I want to help you. I always promised to be there if you needed me and you need me. I just want to know how I can help. I'm good for anything, talking, cleaning, and I've got a great shoulder for leaning on, so talk."

"Everything sucks, and thanks for the offer. I will take you up on a few talks and maybe some cleaning, but there is a silver lining. I just found out I have a brother."

"I've known you since kindergarten. You don't have a brother."

"Mom was pregnant when she met Dad. He loved her, but she had to get rid of the kid. It was a boy. I need to find him. He's all the family I've got." I let her grasp what I'd just told her. "You don't happen to know a good private investigator."

"Oh, I can do better than that."

"You know somebody who can find this guy?"

"Ya, me."

Chapter five

The photo albums I'd have to keep. Mom's pants suits that she'd bought in the seventies I could donate. Dad's ever growing necktie collection was the envy of my Uncle Bob. He could have them. There, I had three piles started. Now all I had to do was sort through the lives of two people and put everything into one of these three piles. There was keep, donate, and give to a family member or friend.

Thankfully I had Eddy with me for most of the morning. He'd dropped by early after talking to Heidi last night. She had told him what I was up to and true to her promise had wanted to help. She'd volunteer Mr Cruiser on the labour end while she did a little digging about this mystery brother.

"Hey, Jon. What about this?" Eddy held up a lamp that hadn't worked in years. It was on Dad's to do list.

"I think you just created a fourth pile. We'll call it the junk pile."

"Fair enough." He set it by the back door. "So what did you do to Heidi? She was so determined to rekindle something with you. Then poof, you're off the table. You got some sex disease or something?"

"I told her about Rebecca. We were supposed to get married. She died the same day my parents did."

"Oh shit. I'm sorry mate. Was she riding with them?"

"No. She was in Paris. It was a different car accident."

"That must have been a rough funeral."

"Don't know. It was the same day as my parent's."

"Man, that's horrible."

"Not really. I don't think I could have handled it. To top it all off, her sister's in the hospital in a coma. I was gonna call, to see how she's doing and apologise for missing the funeral. I couldn't."

"Need me to call them?"

"Nah. I'll do it. I just gotta figure out what I'm going to say to them. I mean, what if Madeline's died since."

"You don't know how she's doing? What hospital is she at?"

"Not sure, but it's past noon and I know you have to get going at noon."

"No big. If I'm late, I'm late."

He walked over to the phone and started dialling numbers. I went back to work sorting clothes and filling a garbage bag with the kind of things that you didn't donate.

"She's still in a coma, but it's an induced coma. They're keeping her in it to give her body a chance to recover. She has a good chance."

"Thanks Mr Cruis… I mean Eddy."

"You can call me cruiser, except I don't have that bike anymore."

"I never knew you hated that name."

"I didn't. Heidi hated it. I thought it was a good name."

"No kidding. You used to cruise the streets and parks on that bike for hours. Whenever I went with you, I had to peddle my ass off to keep up. You had legs on you. You never told me why you cruised so much."

"I was a set of eyes."

"What are you talking about?"

"I had to know what was going on. There was always some drug deal happening in a back alley or in a grove of trees. When your bike was stolen, I knew who took it before the police. When that fire broke out in that garden shed down the street, I knew who started it. It was all useful information back then."

"If you say so." I grabbed a couple of beer from the fridge. "Break time. How do you think Heidi is making out?"

"Are you kidding me? I'd be surprised if she doesn't walk through that door with the guy today. The girl's a pit bull."

"She wouldn't tell me why you guy came to Frankfurt. She's holding onto that lame real estate story."

"Hey." He took his beer. "That was my story."

"What's the real story?"

"It took me hours to come up with that real estate story. I'm sticking with it."

"But it's not anything illegal?"

"I can't talk for her, but that was a lifetime ago for me."

"Fair enough. She said she was a teacher."

"And you believed her?"

"No."

"Good." He finished the beer and set it down. "I should get going. It was nice seeing you again. I hope this isn't goodbye."

"We'll stay in touch this time."

The phone started to ring as he closed the door behind him. I fully expected Heidi with news. It was Marcus.

"Hey, Buddy. You got back okay?"

"Three words; tur-bu-lence. It was like being in an angry massage chair." He switched the phone to the other ear. "So how are you doing?"

"I'm okay. I'm just going through my parent's stuff. They had a lot."

"They had a few years under their belt. I wish I was there to help."

"It's okay. Eddy Cruiser stopped by."

"Say what?"

"Relax. They just wanted to help."

"They?"

"Heidi swung by last night."

"I'm sure she did. Do I have to remind you about…?"

"She's okay. They both are. They've put those years behind them and so have I."

"Well I haven't. We could have been killed. You need to talk to those two and tell them you don't need their help. You especially don't need her help." He fumbled the phone back to his other ear. "Not now, damn it. I'm trying to talk to Jon."

19

"What's going on, Marcus?"

"Inquiring Ingrid wants the scoop." He covered the phone, but I could still hear them. She wanted to know who Heidi was and he was telling her to drop it. "Hey, I gotta go. I swear she was put on this earth to destroy me. Get dressed into the red dress."

"Me," I asked.

"I wish you looked as good as her in that dress. Then I could fire her."

"Isn't love wonderful?" I asked.

"Peachy," he sarcastically answered. "Listen to me, Jon. The woman is trouble. The more distance you put between you and her, the better. Do you hear me, Jon?"

"I hear you." I looked back to see the front door closing. Heidi had let herself in and was quietly standing there. "I knocked but…"

Marcus continued. "If you see her run. If she chases you, run faster. Got it?"

"Got it."

I hung up, walked over and gave her a friendly hug. "That was Marcus. He says hello."

She loosened her grip and leaned back. "Really. I always got the feeling he didn't like me."

"Are you kidding? You guys are good." I made sure my fingers were crossed when I said that. "Did you find anything?"

She opened her jacket and produced an envelope.

Chapter six

Heidi took a seat in the kitchen and I grabbed the chair beside her. I opened the envelope and pulled out two pages. Looking inside, that was all she'd brought. I placed the first page down in front of me and started to read.

She started to talk. "You owe me big for this. I called in a hundred favours."

"His name is Georg?"

"Georg Falkman," she replied.

I kept reading. "A few foster homes."

"Kids are hard to place. Most people want the easy money, you know, teenagers that can take care of themselves. The idea of a baby is good until they start dealing with diapers, baby-proofing the house and bed-wetting. He was definitely a bouncing baby boy."

"Poor kid bounced everywhere in Stuttgart. The report stops when he was four."

"I know. He was transferred to another city, I'm guessing Ludwigsburg. They have a bigger agency and deal with the rural area around Stuttgart."

"Can you find out who picked him up?"

"In time I can find out anything." She scrunched her face. "Now I gotta change gears. How are you feeling?"

"I'm doing okay. This really helps. I can't thank you enough for all your help."

"Like I said, you owe me." Her grin became devilish. "I need two things."

"Name it."

"A bowl of that casserole if there's any left and…"

When she stopped it threw me. This was a girl that was never lost for words—never lost for words, favours, or advice. "You know I have lots. Don't you start getting shy on me now. What's the other thing?"

"Do you have a picture?"

"Of…"

"Of your girlfriend."

"Why do you want to see her?"

Heidi rubbed her nose, more from nerves than an itch. Then her eyes locked on mine. They were sympathetic but wanting. "Maybe if I see her then it will make it more real. I kinda hope it will push you out of my head."

"What are you talking about?"

"When I first saw you in that church I almost lost my lunch. On the drive over to the church I was shaking as if I was detoxing. I couldn't wait to see you."

"You and I haven't seen each other in years, though."

"Doesn't mean I stopped caring."

"But we talked and agreed it was for the best."

"No. You agreed. I never would have let you go, but I had no choice. My hands were tied. My father put a wall between us and I knew you were better off without me, without him, and without all the drama that was my life. Look at you. You cleaned up real nice."

"I never knew."

"After what my father did, I can't blame you. I also couldn't blame you for running out on me. That's why I'm surprised that Marcus said 'hi'. I would have expected him to tell you to run when you see me."

I gave a silent chuckle.

She noticed. "He did say that, didn't he?"

"He did."

"He's still seeing the old me. The old me would have done whatever it took to get you back. That girl is gone, well sorta gone. She's trying to return. That's why I need to see her. The new me will be stronger if I can put a face to the name. Rebecca, right?"

I pulled out my wallet. There was a photo that I always carried. I slipped it out and stared at if for a second before handing it to her. "Yes, it's Rebecca."

She took the picture and studied it as if there was a test. "She's beautiful. You did pretty good for a delinquent from Stuttgart. She's not from around here, is she?"

"Canada. Born in British Columbia."

"Oh, a foreigner. Did she have one of those Canadian accents?"

"She tried not to, but every once in awhile she'd let out an 'eh', or she'd get overly excited about bacon. Oh, and she'd always mispronounce croquets. She'd eat them like they were the greatest thing since the invention of breathing, just couldn't get the name right."

"She sounded amazing."

"That was an understatement."

"Thanks for this."

"For…"

She leaned over and gave me a kiss on the cheek. "Thanks for making her real. I'm trying to be a better person." She held out a hand. "Friends?"

I shook it and nodded. "Friends."

"I can't promise the odd return of the old me. She's a terror and that makes it hard to put the lid on the jar, but I'll do my best."

"And I'll help you."

She pulled out the second page and dropped it on the first. It was a photocopy of a snapshot. The picture was of a very young version of my mother, holding a baby. I looked closer.

"That's Georg?" The photo drew me in as if the child was real. In the folds of blankets held by my mother was the face of my brother. He was a cute little guy.

"It is." She got up to leave. "We'll find him, Jon."

"It's been so many years. He could be anywhere."

"I have a feeling he hasn't strayed far."

23

Chapter seven

That night I stared at the picture of my mother and suddenly couldn't see Georg. He was there, but all I could see was the young woman who brought me into this world. She was a lovely woman and I had to admit, Dad was a lucky man to find a woman so beautiful, so wonderful at taking care of us.

Funny how this house was always so warm, so inviting, and a great place for a child growing up. It was my home. Now it just feels like four walls and a roof. Ingrid and I talked earlier. She thought it might be hard to figure out what I wanted to do with this place. Turns out it was not that hard after all. Without my mother and father, this is just a house. I'd clean it out and list it tomorrow.

What to keep and what to throw out? Maybe I should start calling relatives and get them to swing by and take what they want. I have a cousin that would likely take it all. Some would say she's a hoarder. I think her favourite word is 'free'. Hell, I might just call her first.

I reached for the phone and picked up the receiver. When I went to dial, the only number that came to me was Rebecca's parent's number. I closed my eyes and tried to will it away. It wasn't going anywhere. I dialled the area code and the first four digits of their number before realising I had no idea what I'd say.

Should I tell them the last time we talked it was about wallpaper? Should I tell them we agreed to disagree, something we did a lot when it came to our apartment? Did they need me to tell them she loved them and talked about them often? They knew all that. Did I need to hear that she talked about me? It would be nice, but I knew she loved me.

I dropped the phone in its cradle. Whatever it was they needed to hear, whatever it was I needed to say, it wasn't happening tonight. It would come to me over the next couple of days, hopefully. For now, the books on the shelf behind the television needed to be packed into boxes. I had a co-worker that would love these old classics. I know they couldn't go to a better home.

The boxes I'd picked up from behind Gorges Grocer filled up quickly. I stacked them by the door, sat down on the couch and looked around. My parents had a lot of stuff. I'd definitely need more boxes. Or I could call my cousin and tell her to bring boxes.

A knock on the door got me back to my feet. With any luck it was a relative that needed some furniture or a closet full of clothing. It was Heidi. She had a bottle of wine in her hand that had already been opened.

"Hi. Me again."

"Come in." I stepped back and let her in. "You sharing that wine? I could get us a couple glasses."

"I think that's a great idea." She held up a brown bag. "I also brought strudels."

"Perfect." I grabbed the glasses and returned. "So what brings you back here? You come to help pack? News flash, I ran out of boxes."

"Oh, hell no. I'm not good at packing, moving and…"

"Work in general?"

"You know me too well."

"I just remember you always finding some sucker to do the laborious parts of your life."

"Usually that sucker was you. Sorry about that."

"I never minded." I poured the wine and peeked inside the bag.

"Yes, there's an apple one inside for you."

"Ha." I pulled it out and took a bite. "I missed these. They don't really do Strudels like this in Paris."

This caught her off guard. "You don't live here?"

25

"No. I have an apartment in Paris. It's a little place."

"It sounds nice. I've always wanted to go to Paris." She caught herself. "No, not what I meant. I don't mean for you to take me there. I'd like to go there on my own some day. That wasn't a…"

"Don't worry. Maybe I can take you, show you around. Marcus and Ingrid live there too. We can drop in and say hello."

"Hell, we could do one better and tell them we're dating." She laughed when I didn't. "No. I mean as a joke. I know Marcus would shit himself. That's all I meant, honest."

I let her sweat for a couple seconds before I broke out in laughter. "I'm kidding. I know you meant that. You should have seen the look on your face."

"I forgot how cruel you could be."

"I'm a German boy, through and through."

"I'll say." The tone she used was stuck somewhere between the old Heidi and new one. It was playful, yet innocent.

"The wine is hitting you a little fast," I commented.

"Not really. I started with two bottles."

She shot me a wink. It was the kind that might precede a kiss. The old Heidi was shoving the newer, polite one out of the way. Suddenly she looked as incredible as she did back in the day when we were dating. It was like the years hadn't touched her. She also smelled incredible and that was dangerous. Lately I'd been feeling pretty damned abandoned. Maybe it was the long locks of auburn hair or the twinkle in her eyes when she flirted, but it had my heart racing. I was feeling the passion of our past and the guilt of something that I couldn't let happen. That one was the strongest.

Drunk Heidi moved in for a kiss and that was when I noticed it. Her one eye looked a little different than the other. It didn't jump out at me at first, but soon it couldn't be missed. Heidi had a black eye. It wasn't a full-on black eye yet, but it was on its way. She hadn't had it earlier.

"Whoa. Where'd you get that?"

"Don't change the subject," she slurred.

"I'm serious."

The pucker in her lips melted as she gave up and leaned back. "I don't want to talk about it."

Chapter eight

The eye was darkening by the second. It made me wonder if it had happened on the way over. Sadly it wasn't the first time I'd seen her with a black eye. It used to be a common occurrence.

"Who did this to you?"

"Are you kidding? You know the crowd I hang out with."

"No I don't. You're a teacher and I haven't seen you in what, ten years? I knew the crowd you used to hang out with. That was a long time ago. Surely you don't hang out with those people anymore. Shit, I bet most of them are dead by now."

"First, it's closer to twelve years, and I'm no teacher. Some of the faces have changed but the lifestyles are the same."

"I thought we got away from all that crap."

"Your parents took you away from it. I was left behind at ground zero. We both know my parents weren't going to help me. Shit, my parents were the trouble. I couldn't get free."

"I'm sorry. I just thought…"

"My mother took care of me for a few weeks after Dad left, but she didn't want to. She wanted to escape and find herself. For some reason, she thought she could do that in the bars and taverns. I was doing the Mom stuff and she was doing the brat kid stuff. That was when I ran away and joined the circus."

"The circus?"

"B and E's, cocaine, heroin, sleeping in back alleys or houses when we knew the people were gone on vacation. What would you call it?"

"I'm so sorry. I never knew."

"Don't sweat it. You can make it up to me now." She started to move in for that kiss again.

I countered by getting up. "Come on, Heidi. I just lost Rebecca."

"I'm not asking you to marry me. I just want a kiss."

"You know I can't."

"Ah Johannes, always the nice guy. It gets a little tiring."

I looked over to the door. Could I throw her out? Sounded like a lot of people had given up on her and I was on that list. She caught my glance at the door and got up to leave.

"No. You can't go, not like this. Didn't you come here with Eddy?"

"I'm a big girl. I know my way around the streets. I sure as hell don't need you or him taking care of me."

"You guys get into it? Did he...?"

"What the eye?" She shook her head. "I'd kill Eddy if he ever hit me."

"Did you come to Frankfurt with him?"

"It was more like I followed him. I heard your parents had died and I wanted to come out and see you."

"How'd you hear about them?"

"That's the nice thing about a small town, the old cronies have nothing better to do than talk about the folks that live there, used to live there, and want to live there. Not much to that last category. Regardless, when I found out that Eddy was going I knew that he would lead me here."

"Nothing changes." I tried not to let my disappointment show. It was one of the reasons why I had left. Thing was, she wasn't the problem. Heidi was simply caught up in the muck. I couldn't be mad at her for that. "Look, I can't let you go. The last thing I want is something happening to you."

"Awe, you care."

I knew that was sarcasm, but I didn't care. "Of course I care. You always meant a lot to me. It wasn't your fault I had to split the way I did."

"It wasn't yours either," she confessed.

"I know. It was just a shitty deal. I've learned that life is full of shitty deals."

She took my hand in hers and gave it a gentle squeeze. It was tender and stirred the emotions like a toothpick in a can of paint. I didn't want to acknowledge it yet when her eyes met mine, that toothpick had turned into a wooden spoon. "Stop it."

"I would if you really wanted me to." She moved in closer. "But you don't want that."

I took a step back. "I think I do."

"Nah. You want to forget the pain. You want a moment that doesn't tear you up inside. You want to feel my passion like you used to. It was always so magical, wasn't it?"

It was magical. I couldn't deny that. I also couldn't admit it.

"Come on Jon. There isn't one reason why you shouldn't be happy. I know I could be your happy place."

My happy place? I tried to pull my eyes away. I couldn't. This girl was hard to ignore and everything she said was right. A moment wouldn't hurt anybody. Rebecca was dead. "I'm just not ready yet."

She smiled, leaned in and gave me a tender kiss on the lips. It was brief, but the affection lingered like an expensive perfume. It filled my senses and brought back all those memories of us being young and in love.

"I can't, Heidi."

"I know. You're a good man. I'm gonna go." She put her arms out and twirled a drunken spin. "Ta-Da. The new Heidi has returned."

"No, you need to stay. Somebody hit you, your drunk, and I'm tired of seeing you get the short straw. You deserve better. You can sleep in my bed."

"Seriously?" Her eyes widened.

"Sure. I'll sleep in my parent's room."

Her shoulders slumped as she sat back down on the couch and reached for the wine bottle. "Oh."

"How about I get some of Aunt Trudy's gingersnaps while you concoct a story to explain why a German real estate agent, who is also a teacher, has a shiner."

"Can I start it with, 'Once upon a time'?"

"You can start it with what ever you want. May I suggest you add an old woman and a baby carriage full of chickens?"

She laughed like she had years ago, years when we were kids and didn't have this thing called life hanging over our heads. As the evening rolled along there was more laughing, a few tears and more emotions stirred. She had always been a good kid and as a teenager, simply misunderstood. So who was she now?

Ever the gentleman, I had offered the auburn-haired beauty my bed and she had taken it. This girl had proven to be a regular Jekyll and Hyde. Her drunk flirting and lonely advances were always countered with a slurred apology that only the new and improved Heidi could give.

But at some point during the night there had been a relapse. When I woke up, I had the old Heidi wrapped around me like an anaconda. She was naked, and she was snoring.

Chapter nine

My arm was caught under her and our legs were a tangle of limbs. How did she do this? I tried to figure an escape route, but she had me pinned pretty good. So should I wake her? No longer drunk, she'd be the new Heidi and as embarrassed as I was.

I quietly cleared my throat. Heidi returned another snort. When I cleared my throat a little louder, she grunted and nuzzled closer. That was when I realised I'd gone to sleep without a shirt or pants and her front was pressed against me. It was horrible at first, washing me with guilt, but as the minutes passed, so did the guilt. After a handful of minutes I was more curious. Her breasts seemed a lot fuller than I remembered. I had to look down. Heidi had grown at least a cup size since her teens. It didn't stir any emotions, but it did get somebody else's attention. I had to roll over a bit to give him room. I didn't need him growing against her hip. If that woke her up I'd never be able to explain it.

When I moved, she also stirred, rolling onto her back. She'd definitely grown a full cup size. I tried to look away but couldn't.

Her eyes opened while I was still staring. "What the hell, Jon?" She immediately worked her arms free and crossed them across her chest.

"What did I do? You crawled into bed with me."

"After you got me drunk."

"I never got you…"

31

She broke into hearty laughter. "I am so sorry, but I wish you could see the look on your face."

I was wrong. There was no embarrassment. She untangled herself, got up and sauntered back to her bedroom where she'd left her clothing. It was a smouldering walk and I didn't look away. I wanted to, but this girl's butt was devilishly good at holding a man's attention.

My pants were hanging on the end of the bed and I slipped them on both legs at once. The shirt quickly followed. With that smooth-skinned hourglass out of sight I could refocus. I didn't need this and neither did she.

"You want eggs?" I asked as I made my way to the kitchen.

Her head poked out of the bedroom. "Scrambled with ketchup?"

"Sure."

She disappeared for a second and returned dressed. "Can I make French toast?"

"Really? I don't have maple syrup."

"That's fine. We can use butter, sprinkled with cinnamon and icing sugar. That's what we used when we were kids, remember?"

"I remember that. Your parents had an old salt and pepper shaker, cinnamon in one and icing sugar in the other. What did you call that?"

"I think I called it Welfare toast, only because they were too damn cheap to buy maple syrup."

"My parents were cheap too. They made syrup out of water, brown sugar, vanilla and butter. It wasn't maple syrup, but it was good." Then I remembered. "Sandbox toast. That's what you called it."

She frowned as she got a bowl and broke an egg into it. "I vaguely remember that, but it wasn't me that called it that."

"It was Fast Eddy. He used to prefer real sugar."

"That's right." She dipped the first slice of bread into the egg and dropped it in the pan. "Weirdo never liked icing sugar."

I continued to stir the scrambled eggs. "That was grade eight, wasn't it?"

"Seven," Heidi corrected. "In grade eight, Eddy's foster parents got a microwave oven and we discovered popcorn. We used to make so much of it our bellies hurt."

"We spent our paper route money on those big bags of the stuff."

"Most kids bought candy and comic books. We bought popcorn and butter. We were a touch loco."

It dragged me down memory lane. There was the jumping garbage cans with our bicycles, the short stint with home-made gunpowder, and the time we dared each other to jump onto a moving train and take it to Munich. "Do you remember Munich?"

She put the first slice of french toast on a plate and dropped the second in the pan. "I was fourteen, it was a warm summer evening, and I spent it in a cattle car with you, Eddy and eight rather large pigs."

"Do you remember why we went there?"

"The museum," she replied as she found the butter and cinnamon. "I had a book report and we thought we could steal something to get me an A. I wasn't the best student so I needed the help."

"Did we get you anything?"

"No. We set off an alarm, ran like hell and hopped the first train back. I got my first kiss that day."

"Oh. From who?"

"You're such an ass." She abruptly flipped the second slice of french toast in the pan and it broke. "This one is yours."

"I kissed you?"

"You don't remember? We were on a railcar that was hauling vehicles. We broke into a BMW and Eddy fell asleep in the backseat. We were playing the what-if game and I asked you what-if I kissed you. I was hoping you'd get the hint, but you were shy. I mean you were willing to steal shit from a museum with me, but a kiss, that was too risky."

"We didn't steal anything."

"But we tried." She dropped the second piece of toast on a different plate. "Those eggs ready?"

I scooped some on her plate, some on mine. Then I grabbed the ketchup and headed for the table. "You kissed me, didn't you?"

"I'd have been an old lady waiting for you to make a move." She took the two plates to the table and sat down. "Wanna do supper tonight?"

"Sure. Hey, didn't we start dating that night?"

"Dated until you and Marcus moved away." Then as casually as she could, she added, "So how long did you know Rebecca?"

"Oh I get it. I only knew Rebecca a couple years and yet I've known you like ten."

"Do the math Einstein. You've known me a lifetime."

"I agree. So what do you want from me? You want to pick up where we left off, maybe we set a wedding date?"

"Don't be such a drama queen, Jon. I don't want you to be scared of me. You and I have been through a lot and I don't want to deny the feelings I have for you. You shouldn't be afraid to see if you have any. We were always a good team."

"I just lost the woman I was about to marry."

"I'm not saying you don't grieve, and you shouldn't forget her either. Just don't write me off. I might be something you'll want to pursue when the time is right."

"Maybe. I just don't know if the time will ever be right again."

"You're hurting right now, but in time that'll pass. I don't see somebody like you spending the rest of your life alone. You need to be a father, a husband, and a grandfather. I think I'd make an awesome gramma. I've already got french toast dialled in."

"Mine was broken."

She looked up and flipped her eyebrows. "Don't piss off gramma next time."

I watched as she picked away at her eggs. She was beautiful, compassionate and I knew she'd never hurt me. As a teenager she had loved me like a stray puppy and would have followed me anywhere, had I let her. Thing was, I hadn't let her. She'd been left behind. Why had I done that? Then I remembered.

It was Joseph.

Chapter ten

B ack at the lawyer's office there were papers to sign and further instructions on a few of Dad's pension funds. I sat in the office with my mind bouncing between Rebecca, who I missed horribly, and Heidi, who had wormed her way into my thoughts in a way that both bothered and comforted me.

When thing were bad, just before I left Stuttgart, we had shared many a sleepless night playing the what-if game. What-if we just ran off, what-if we turned ourselves into the police, and what-if one of us gets caught. I'd never played the game since, until now.

"I think we're done here." Mr Krandle announced. "Again, I'm sorry for your loss, Jon."

"Thank you."

I stepped out into the street and didn't make it twenty steps before hearing a familiar voice.

"Johannes."

I turned to see Fast Eddy Cruiser. He was wearing his usual soccer hooligan outfit, worn t-shirt and jeans. "Hey Eddy."

"Good to see you again. Wasn't sure we'd run into each other. What ya doing down here?"

"Lawyer stuff," I answered.

His chipper mood softened. "Oh. Sorry about all that."

"Hey, I got the chance to run into you guys."

"Yes. It's been a while. Can I buy you a beer and a brat? We can catch up."

"There's a pub around the corner. You still play crib?"

"Ludwigsburg champion," He boasted.

We stepped into the bar and while he bought the beer, I signed out the board and the cards. There was a table in the corner and we both gravitated toward it. We'd learned as teens that the corners were the safest.

"Cut for deal?"

I cut an ace to his three and I started to shuffle. "So you let Heidi tag along. That was nice of you."

"Ya lost me," he answered as he set up the pegs.

"She said you read about my parents and planned to come out to pay your respects. She said she tagged along."

With a mouthful of beer he picked up his cards. "First of all. I don't live anywhere near her. Second, I ran into her in Frankfurt. She was the one who told me about your parents." He picked two cards and tossed them my way. "And thirdly, when did you find all this out?"

I placed two cards from my hand with the two he gave me. "I ran into her yesterday, well, last night."

"That bird'll never change. She's always got an angle. Four." He put the four of diamonds down. "Did she tell you that real estate shit was her idea?"

I set a queen down for ten more and took a drink. "I figured that out on my own. So where do you live?"

"Sorry my friend." He dropped an ace and pegged the two points. "That is privileged information. Since we all went our separate ways, I keep a tight lid on everything I do. I just don't trust *him*."

It was the way he said *him*, like it was a name that couldn't be mentioned without serious repercussion. I dropped my one-eyed jack down for twenty-five and took another swig of beer. "Him, is in jail."

"I don't care." He had a six for two more points. "That guy is evil or don't you remember?"

"I seem to have forgotten a good chunk of it." I put a four down and he countered with another one and triumphantly lifted his mug before pegging two more points.

"That's eight for two more."

"Horseshoes." I dropped my last card, an ace, for nine.

"You're forgetting, and that's the Heidi affect." He set his five down for last card and a single point. "She looks good and uses the rainbows of her beauty to hide the shit storms. You remember why we all took off, right?"

"That was Joseph."

"Right. When he went to prison, we all took the opportunity to make new lives for ourselves. Heidi stayed behind."

"How do you know?" I watched as he reached for the deck and cut the cards. I reached for my beer.

"I've kept track of all of you. Marcus became a photographer and moved to Paris shortly after you settled in there. You work as a finishing carpenter and Heidi, she's messed up in some of her father's business."

"That would explain the shiner." I reached to flip the top card hoping for an ace or a four.

"Don't let her bring that shit into your world, man. You don't need that."

I threw the card down face up. It was a five which helped me a little, helped him a lot.

"Ouch." He fanned his cards on the table and started counting his twelve points out loud. Then he pegged them. "You didn't need that either."

I counted out and pegged my four points. Heidi had spent the night. I couldn't tell Eddy that. His suspicions were already in overdrive. That being said, it was sure convenient that she dropped by and found her way into my bed. Had she searched my room, was she setting me up?

"You didn't…"

"No way." It hurt that he could think such a thing, but in his defence, she had come, stayed, and ended up naked, curled up against me. It wasn't from a lack of trying on her part.

"Good. She's a delicious treat, but she'll rot ya quicker than sugar. You don't want that."

He was right about that. He was also right about Joseph. The man was dangerous and he had an axe to bury. "You said you'd been spying on all of us?"

Eddy took a drink, rounded up the cards, and started to shuffle. "Call it what you want, spying, looking out for, keeping in touch. After Joseph went to jail we had the smarts to run. I took it one step further and decided to be proactive. I'm looking out for us. Did you know he gets out next year?"

"He what?" That sent a shiver up my spine. I wasn't afraid of the man when he was behind bars. Being free and out there somewhere, that changed everything.

"Doesn't surprise me that Heidi didn't tell you." He started to deal the next hand. "Ask her about him, next time you see her."

That would be tonight. I downed the rest of my beer and flagged the waitress for a couple more.

Chapter eleven

I was half cut by the time I got home. Fast Eddy Cruiser had taken all three games of crib, which meant I bought the beer. I'd eaten, a Brat and fries, but I was still hungry. I walked over to the freezer and opened the door. There was a choice of seven different casseroles and I picked one with ham, cheese and mashed potatoes. I also took out some lemon squares.

Heidi was punctual, saying she'd pop by at six. The knocking on the door started a minute after. I opened it and had to remind myself to breathe. Her stilettos, fishnet stockings, mini skirt and white blouse that revealed a dangerous amount of cleavage, left me speechless.

She stepped past me. "You look good and the food smells delicious."

Leaving her shoes on, she pranced toward the kitchen like a thoroughbred. My eyes followed her and had me thinking about earlier, when she did a similar walk in her birthday suit. I pushed the image away, eventually. "I hope you're okay with ham and potatoes."

"You remembered that I love ham. See, I knew you cared."

I had a feeling I should have grabbed something with hamburger. This wasn't a date and I didn't want her thinking I'd put a lot of thought into it. "Just the top dish in the freezer."

"Fair enough. I brought six Bierre Hans. You remember these things?"

"Oh, wow. I didn't know that brewery was still in business. I love this beer."

"Really? I only grabbed them because they were the closest to the cash register."

I gave her a chuckle. "You got me there."

"There's nothing wrong with me picking the beer you like, or you cooking something I might enjoy." The beers had a spring top so she popped one open. "It was one of these beers that knocked my tooth out."

"I think it was you that knocked your tooth out. That, and drinking under the school bleachers when we were supposed to be in math class."

"That's right. I tripped and damn near swallowed the darn thing."

I opened one for myself and took a swig. "You bled like I'd never seen before."

"But not as bad as when I took a tumble through that barbed wire fence. I got in so much shit for that."

"For stealing chocolate bars or for getting hurt?"

"For ruining my new jeans and getting blood on the carpet at home." She turned, lifted her skirt, and exposed a hip with a cluster of three-inch scars. "Battle wounds from a ten year old."

This time I took a long look at the faint scars on her hip. The scars were nothing like I remembered. "Okay little miss exhibitionist. Show me your other hip."

She spun and flipped the other side of her skirt. "You like what you see?"

There was the scar I remembered. "That's the barbed wire scar. What were the other ones from?"

Quickly checking both hips with her own eyes she began to blush. "Nothing."

"They sure looked like something."

She shook her head and tugged her skirt down as if instantly ashamed of her body. "Let's forget it. How's supper coming?"

"Were those from your Dad?"

"Can we not talk about him?"

40

"Do you see him often? Eddy says you're running part of the family business. Do you do that from your schoolhouse?"

"Eddy has a big mouth and what part of 'I don't want to talk about this' did you not understand?"

"We can do this two ways. We can talk about it over supper like two adults, or I can get you drunk and wait for you to spill your guts."

She put the beer down. "I hate that man. You know that, but he's my father. I used to see him once a week. It took me a year to do that first visit. That was when he asked a favour."

"After all he did to us?"

"I said yes to him."

"What did he ask?"

"He asked me to take over the business. He gave me a couple of names for leveraging my competitors."

"Why'd you agree, Heidi?"

"My Dad was never perfect, but he had standards. When he went to jail, others moved in and they sold whatever to whoever. Drugs were running through the schools like wind through the trees in November. Nobody, including the police, expected such an influx of crime."

"So your father…"

"The man was a beast, but as long as he was in charge it was on his terms and nothing was sold to kids. It was a free for all until I got things running again. I had to muscle a few people out of town, but soon the crime wave subsided. The police came to see me and almost gave me their blessing. They'd never touch me as long as I could keep a lid on the others."

"So why'd you come to Frankfurt. You see that's the other thing Eddy told me. He doesn't live in Stuttgart anymore and hasn't been in touch in quite some time. You told me you followed him out here."

"I did. He just didn't know."

"You've been spying on…"

"It was the least I could do."

"What do you mean?"

She picked up her beer, downed the lion's share and let her eyes fall into mine. "I came here to warn you."

41

"Your Dad is out?"

"He got out yesterday."

"How'd you find me?"

"I have people. Actually I had the police find you. They do favours for me, and I give donations to them. It's the perfect system, or at least it was."

"Is that why the shiner?"

"My father wants me home, says I shouldn't be consorting with the police. The guy that did this underestimated me, but Dad will send more. I know he's planning his revenge. I don't want you getting caught up in that. I can get you false ID's, money, whatever you need. I just want you gone. If you can get out of the country, that would be best. The police don't want trouble with foreign countries."

"I live in France."

"That's perfect. You should go. Take Idiot Eddy with you."

"I'll tell him Joseph is out. That should do it." I took her hand and pulled her in for a hug. "You're shaking like a leaf."

The hug was returned, but she was shaking. "I can handle him. I just couldn't handle anything happening to you."

"I should have taken the fall. I was a teenager. I would have got a slap on the wrist, a fine and a few community hours."

"Why didn't you?"

She knew the answer to that. Had I taken the fall he'd be free to continue his brutal abuse of his daughter. Heidi had become the reason for anything bad that happened. It became normal to see her with a fat lip or black eye. The bruises on her wrists, arms and neck never faded.

"He had to be stopped."

She looked up and kissed my cheek. "You were my hero by keeping quiet. You'd saved me by having that man locked away. I'll always owe you for that."

"But he's out."

"He is. For that reason, I want you on a plane tomorrow. Can you do that for me?"

"What are you going to do?"

"Hang out in Frankfurt for a few days. Maybe a solution will come to me."

"And if they find you again?"

She began to tremble harder.

"I'll take my parent's room, you can have mine," I offered. "Can you stay put this time?"

She smiled and I wasn't sure how to take that.

Chapter twelve

S omething told me that if I hung out in front of my lawyer's office long enough, Eddy would cruise by. He said he was staying in the area. Besides, it was a little past noon, which meant that soccer was on the television somewhere and the beer was flowing.

His characteristic worn t-shirts stood out in a crowd. "There you are."

"You back for more punishment, Jon?"

"Don't feel much like cards, but I'll let you buy me a beer. I ran into Heidi after I left the pub."

"Sounds serious."

"It is." I walked ahead of him and grabbed a corner table. This time it was more out of purpose than habit.

"You talked to her about her father, didn't you?"

"I did." The waitress came with two beers and I let Eddy pay. "Joseph isn't getting out in a year."

"Really? That's wonderful."

"Not really. He got out yesterday. That's why she's here. She was trying to find a way to tell us."

"One second." He got up, took his phone out of his pocket and speed dialled someone. Then he started for the other corner of the bar. There was no purpose in walking there. Like an expectant father, he was pacing. He talked for a few seconds and hung up as he made his way back to me. "Got a guy that's going to check that out. Courts don't have him free until next year."

"Ya, well his daughter is doing such a good job running the business that they've probably given him time off for her good behaviour."

"I knew she was running the show. She had no choice."

"That's our Heidi, no fear." I held back the bit about the hug and her shaking like the San Andreas Fault. "How are you getting confirmation?"

"I still have eyes and ears in Stuttgart."

"You don't think that's overkill?"

"Don't be too obvious, but look across the bar." He waited. "See the guy by the door, sitting alone and looking over every ten seconds?"

"I do now. You know him?"

"I'm a betting man. I'll put the price of my airline ticket on him following you into the john. Get up and go. If I'm wrong, I'll buy your ticket."

I took a quick peek back at the guy. The man looked harmless. "You're just being paranoid."

"Look, Jon. We used to move dope, cocaine, and whatever else that was in those packages. We moved a lot for Joseph, did a good job, and we got paid. Part of our salary, albeit it implied and never spoken, was that we'd take the fall for him if needed. We were teens and we all knew the worst they could do is slap our pee pees. Well, our protection was needed and we let him fry. The man got twelve years. Don't think for a second that he's okay with that."

"I guess."

The phone rang and was quickly answered. "Yes... okay... thanks. We have to leave."

"Why?"

"He got out yesterday and he's not in Stuttgart anymore. You know what that means."

"It means Heidi was right. She wants us to get out of the country. How long do you think we have?"

"Get up and go to the john."

"But I don't have to go."

"Humour me, and don't look over to that guy."

I shrugged, got up, downed my beer and made my way to the bathroom. As far as I was concerned, it was worth a free flight.

Turned out I had to go after all. I chose my urinal, did my business and zipped up. I was headed to the sink and thinking about the window seat when I was shoved up against the wall. I hadn't heard him enter the room.

The voice was rough. "Got a guy that wants to see you."

"I think you have the wrong…"

My wrist was pulled behind my back and shoved upward. "You screwed him. Now he wants to return the favour."

The man wasn't big, smaller than I was, yet I couldn't leverage myself free. The harder I fought, the more he wrapped me up. "Where is he?"

"He's waiting back at the apartment. You're going to go back to the table and tell your friend that you remembered you have to do something. Then you'll leave and I'll follow you out. Got it?"

"And if I don't?"

He pulled me away from the wall and slammed me back into it. My head bounced off the stained tiles and I saw stars. Then, just like that, he let go of me. I spun to ready myself for his next attack when I saw Eddy taking the man to the ground. He landed face down with my friend on his back. Eddy's fist found the side of the man's head followed by three more quick shots.

I headed over to help, but Eddy didn't need any. He spun the man on his back and fed him two more shots. "Change of plans, buddy. Here's how it's gonna work. You'll leave without my friend, you'll tell Joseph to drop this, and we'll never see each other again. Got it?"

"You have no idea what you're starting."

"Oh, I think I do. Now I'm gonna get up and so are you. Then you're going to leave."

The man got up and headed for the door. "We'll be back. You have to know that."

Eddy held his arms out. He didn't care. "We'll be waiting."

I waited for the door to close behind him. "We will?"

"Hell, no." He dialled the airlines. "Paris works for you, doesn't it, Jon?"

"It does." I picked a credit card out of my wallet and handed it over. "Can I at least have the window seat?"

Eddy shook the blood from his knuckles. "Not a chance."

Chapter thirteen

Paris, France

The plane landed at Charles De Gaulle Airport after a short but tumultuous flight. I ended up with the window seat and saw white clouds all the way in. Paris was getting its usual rain. Eddy and I pulled our carry-ons out of the overhead luggage compartments and slowly made our way off the plane.

I tried again. "Where in Paris do you live?"

Eddy didn't bite. "Not to worry. Hey you wanna have a beer?"

"I'm okay. So you're never going back?"

"No need. I live here now and so do you. I doubt he'll chase us this far."

"And we just say good-bye to our past."

"Now you're getting it." He worked his way down the near empty airport to the Metro. "Gare du Nord station?"

I followed beside him. "Yes, but you already knew that didn't you?"

"Look, I trust very few people these days. It's no offence." He reached into his pocket and grabbed a pen. Then he scribbled a number on a scrap piece of paper. "I'm always up for a beer or a game of crib. Call me some time."

I slipped the number in a pocket and paid for both Metro passes. The airport wasn't busy, nor was the Metro. I usually travelled weekends and fought crowds. It was nice to have a choice of seats.

"So what now," I asked.

"Life. Forget about Germany. Forget about Heidi and Joseph. None of that exists anymore in this world. Imagine we just stepped off a time machine."

"Kinda hard." I watched the stops as the lights on the map lit up.

"Not when you think about it."

But I was thinking about it. I was thinking about the friend that I'd known since grade two. She had stolen chocolate bars with me, taught me to dance, gave me my first kiss, taken my virginity. I had taken hers. We were more than that though. She was always there for me, staying with me when I had the measles, finding out that my brother's name was Georg Falkman. She had pulled strings for me to acquire a picture of him. She'd been beaten up and still braved warning me about her father. Did I say goodbye to her this morning?

The Republic stop was the next one and I got up. "Thanks for everything, Eddy."

"Don't be a stranger."

The doors opened and I walked away.

Instead of going home, I headed for the train heading east. I'd take it to Père Lachaise station and walk the rest of the way. Dragging my carry-on behind me I made my way along the sidewalk and through the pathways. The cemetery was just up ahead.

A grounds-keeper had parked his tractor by a large tree and was cleaning up a flowerbed. I walked over to him. "*Excusez-moi.*"

"*Bonjour.*" He stopped and clapped the dirt off his gloves.

"*Je cherche quelqu'un.*"

My French was a lot worse than his English. He replied, "Who are you looking for?"

"She would have been buried here a few days ago." I swallowed my next breath. "Rebecca Harrows."

He nodded and respectfully dropped his head as he walked away. I kept three feet back and fought my emotions as the tears dared their escape. This was real. She was buried her. She was gone.

The man stopped at a patch of grass that had been set down like a poorly sewn quilt. I nodded my thanks and the man left me alone.

Dropping to my knees I started putting the grass into neater squares. I matched corners and worked the seams into each other properly. When I was done it looked like a well-manicured lawn, albeit lumpy. I couldn't hold the tears back any longer.

My Rebecca was in a coffin, six feet below this grass. She wasn't breathing anymore. A car accident had taken her from me. It was still hard to believe she was there. How did they know this wasn't the grave of somebody else? There was no tombstone, no marker of any kind. What if they got it wrong?

Then I saw the little grave marker. It was a temporary paper tag, tucked in a metal frame with a prong that stuck it into the ground. It was hand-written, more a chicken scratch.

I immediately got to my feet and looked around. The flowerbeds were lush, abundant, and almost over-abundant. Red and white flowers would have been Rebecca's favourite, so I made a bouquet from the flowers I picked. I set them beside her tag and smiled through tears that stung like battery acid.

Suddenly I didn't want to go back to the apartment. What if she had clothing sitting out? Could I handle seeing anything of her things right now? She made the throw pillows on the couch. Had she bought that awful wallpaper? Maybe it was sitting on the dining room table. What was the last thing she did?

I definitely didn't want to go back to the apartment yet.

"What were you thinking, Babe?" I asked her. "We were supposed to grow old together. I'm not mad, but we should have talked about this. We needed to talk about this. I wanted to die an old man, and I wanted to go first. Maybe I'd have a heart attack after eating some of your lousy cooking. You'd rush over and I'd tell you I love you. You'd hold me and tell me you love me too. Then I'd be gone."

I got to my feet. "I guess I am mad at you, Darling. Don't expect me to get over this."

My hand fluttered toward my carry-on, which was actually my father's, until I found the handle. "I've got to go now. I have a brother to find and a friend to take care of. I know you'll understand, and if you don't, then we can be mad at each other for a while."

Wiping at my eyes with my free hand, I walked away.

I stopped at the edge of the grass and looked back. "Just know that mad or not, I'll always love you."

Back through the pathways, I made my way to the Metro. I couldn't stay here. There was nothing for me here. With Rebecca gone, my life was an empty glass.

Sitting on the train, I stared blankly at the drops clinging to the window and at the dampness in the streets. Paris was such a dismal place. It always rained here. Sure there was history, but it was a history of death. From the statues and paintings of people no longer with us to the six million buried in the catacombs, Paris was nothing more than a chronicle of heartbreak. Who needed that?

The train rolled through the city as it returned me to Charles de Gaulle Airport. I made my way to the Air France window. "When's the next flight to Frankfurt?"

Chapter fourteen

Frankfurt, Germany

I woke up back in Germany to a woodpecker hammering a hole into a power pole. The sun was shining and my stomach was growling. Breakfast would be the potato and ham casserole. I was in a good mood, all things considered. The idea that Rebecca was actually gone was starting to settle in my mind. I think seeing her grave and saying goodbye was what I needed. She'll always be my love, but I have to put my head down and continue on with life. I'd just lost my parents and needed to do something with this house. And then there was Joseph and the task of finding my brother. At least it wasn't raining.

My first order of business was to get this house listed. I had already dropped off a key with my uncle. His neighbour was a real-estate agent and eager to list it. They'd pop by today and hammer a sign in the front lawn.

Me, I'd head out the back door and run down to Römer Square. With any luck I'd run into Heidi. With any luck she'd still be willing to help me find Georg. She had mentioned that she was staying in a hotel down in Old Sachsenhausen. She'd also said she wasn't going back right away.

Römer Square was quiet. There were a few kiosks open and the restaurants, but there was no Heidi. Down by the water and across the bridge I was entering the older section of Frankfurt. Old Sachsenhausen was a handful of blocks and mostly shopping, restaurants, and hotels. I don't know what I was thinking just showing up without a plan. There was a good chance I'd find nothing more than a good meal. What was my plan, go knocking on doors asking if anybody had seen an auburn-haired woman with racoon eyes? That being said, they'd know it if they'd seen her.

I strolled a few blocks and was content killing time. There was no urgency right now. Maybe if I saw Joseph I'd have a reason to run or hide but I couldn't even find him.

I'd just started walking the back alleys when an old lady spat at me. That old lady, half-hidden down a dead-end driveway, was one that had been spitting on tourists for years. The driveway might have been a gravel loading dock at one time. Made of cement, the old stout woman shot water from her mouth every thirty seconds. She had caught many a tourist as they walked by.

The shot of water hitting me in the leg was a welcome distraction and I almost missed the girl sitting at the far corner of the lot. She had her head buried in a book. She didn't see me as I moved in closer.

"Good book?"

Heidi looked up as if she was about to be shot at. "Oh my God, it's you. Don't scare me like that. What the hell are you doing here? I thought you left."

"I left, visited Rebecca's grave and came back. You see, with my parents gone and Rebecca dead, I'm running out of friends."

"What about Marcus?"

"He's busy with Ingrid."

"You came back for me?"

"And my brother, so don't go seeing something that isn't there. You and I have history. I can't walk away while that animal is out there." I held my hand out for her to take.

"You mean my father?" She took it and let me lift her up.

"Call him what you want. I don't want him hurting you again." I motioned to the black eye. It wasn't looking any better.

"I'd hate to think of what he'll do to you when he catches you. You know he's got eyes everywhere."

"He already sent a guy to collect me. Didn't work. I think he was following Eddy."

"Only to get to you. You're the one he blames, and me. He's kinda mad at Marcus and has no respect for Eddy, but those two don't warrant the energy to swing a fist."

"Obviously you do." I pointed to a restaurant. "Shall we grab a bite?"

She winked with the darker eye. "I'd love to do lunch."

"So your father's still mad at you?"

"Furious. I think he wanted to put me in a hospital. I dove through a window to get away. And then you beat up one of his thugs. We might have to share a room at the hospital."

"Not funny."

"Yet here you are back in Frankfurt."

We walked into the one restaurant and the waiter offered us a spot outside at one of the long tables. We declined and made our way to the back where we found a quiet booth.

"I still have to find my brother. Think you can help?"

"I might be able to pull a few more strings, but you don't get to go with me when I do. These people trust me, hate outsiders."

"Where are you staying?"

"I don't have a place. It was my own hotel window that I jumped through when they found me."

"Was it at least open?"

She pulled a sleeve back to reveal a nasty cut that should have had stitches. "Would have been easier."

"Damn."

She pulled her sleeve down when the waitress came by. "Beer and a schnitzel please." She turned to me. "Two?"

"Sounds good. A good wheat beer."

She nodded, jotted the order on her notepad and left.

"I can pay, Heidi."

"I'm good." She reached down her blouse and flashed a wad of cash that was rolled up with an elastic band. "My fee for running his business all those years."

"Like that wasn't a reason to hit you."

"I doubt he knows about this yet. He hit me because I was one of the kids that should have kept him from going to jail." She took the beer from the waitress when she arrived.

I took the other one before it hit the table.

Heidi downed a long mouthful and then pulled out her phone. "Jack, it's me. You know that favour you did for me? I need you to dig a little deeper. I'll pay. Yes. Yes. Okay, I'll give you four hours and thanks. This means a lot to me. Right. Say hello to Jane for me. Thanks again. Bye." She set the phone down beside her beer. "My people are on it."

"Your people? I thought they were his now."

"Some transition slower than others."

Chapter fifteen

After the meal we got up, paid and stepped outside. The clouds had shrouded the sun. Shadows from the large trees were lost in the gloom. I looked up to see that rain was on the way. I wasn't paying attention to the streets. Heidi was. She latched onto my wrist and dragged me across the street. Cars locked up brakes as we wove our way to the other side. We'd been made. Two guys that must have been track stars in a previous life were right behind us.

Heidi let go of my wrist and led the way. I wilfully followed. She was only five foot five yet she was leaving me behind. Good thing, because when she darted right I had time to do the same. If I were closer, she'd likely zig and I'd zag. She almost lost me when she ducked into a butcher's shop.

"What are we doing in here?"

"Watch and learn." She ushered me inside the meat locker and shut the door behind her. "Pull on the latch so he can't open it."

The man behind the counter didn't have the chance to stop us. He started pounding on the door first. It startled me.

"Why here?" I asked. "They know we're going to have to come out of here soon enough. It's too cold in here."

"That's what I'm counting on."

Soon three sets of hands were beating on the door. I held on for all I was worth while she picked a frozen ham and brought it over. Then she lifted it up and jammed it against the lock. "You can let go now."

"Are you sure?"

"That'll hold until it either thaws or until they figure out they'll have to pop the hinge pins to get this door open."

"How do you know this?"

"This isn't my first rodeo, Jon." She started tapping at wall panels. "Okay. I might have been trapped in a meat locker once. I got out of it due to a panic that gave me nightmares for months."

"Who locked you in there?"

"Let's just say not all guys are as sweet as you." She found the panel she wanted and dug into her pocket for a couple of thin coins. One of the coins was handed to me. "Start unscrewing."

"Why are we…?"

"Talk and work. It will only take them ten minutes to pop those hinges, once they decide to do it. I'll bet they're already on it."

"Is this a wall to outside?"

"I need you to unscrew."

Three screws hit the floor by her hands and two by mine. There were twelve in all and I felt that this wall didn't lead outside. By the time the eighth screw hit the floor, the bottom hinge had been popped.

"Shit. Hurry up old man."

"Old man?"

"That's how you're screwing. We've got five minutes to be a block away so pick up the pace."

When the twelfth screw hit the ground I could proudly say that I had picked up the pace and got six of them. Heidi didn't care about that. She was still trying to save us.

There was a hollow between the interior and exterior walls. "What is this?"

"Every meat locker has one main culprit." She started to shove me in the wall. "That's bacteria. Now climb."

"Bacteria?" I reluctantly started to climb through the opening. She got underneath me and helped by shoving me upward. I reached the ceiling part of the duct and climbed into it. "This will hold me?"

"Yes. Do you see a fan?"

"Across, on the other side."

"Pitter patter. This is a condensation system. It prevents moisture build up."

I made my way to the fan. "Moisture is water, water is bacteria?"

"You're learning." She came up behind me. "Okay, time to get rid of the fan. The free world is on the other side."

I looked at the four screws holding it in place. "I don't have my coin. Do you have another?"

"Here's a thought." She butted up against me. "Be a man and kick the damn thing out."

"Sure. I can do that."

I pulled my legs in and Heidi braced herself. When I kicked, she slid back and the fan took a solid impact. As I recoiled, she shoved me closer and locked herself in place. The fan hung loosely on three screws and had stopped spinning. I kicked again and the fan dropped into the back alley. I wanted to lower myself down, but Heidi was shoving for all she was worth. I popped out of the hole like wad of wet paper from of a child's spitball straw.

I landed with a thud. Heidi landed on top of me.

"I'm pretty sure I heard the other hinge pop." She started for the street.

I grabbed her by the arm and dragged her into the nearest hotel. "This is the last thing they'd expect."

"Because it's crazy." She thought about it and shrugged. "It might work."

While we headed for the front desk, she gave me a story. I was a married man with a wife and three children. They were off shopping. My daughter had lost her suitcase and they needed to pick up a few things, underwear, toothbrush, and other kid things. Heidi promised to meet me on the stairs leading up to the second floor. I'd have to sell the daughter story because they'd be canvassing, looking for a man and a woman. They wouldn't be looking for children.

"Whatever you do. Don't give them a real name and pay with cash, but be cheap and try to get a deal on the room. Buy three days, not one. We are not hiding out. We're a family on vacation.

Ask them about the sights, for the kids. Maybe they could recommend a good place to eat. Your son doesn't like seafood. You got all that?"

"My name is Paul and my overbearing wife is Bertha. She used to be a looker, but lately she's let herself go. Three kids later and I'm wishing I was dead. If he's married he'll understand."

"Don't oversell. She's probably cute as hell and you couldn't do any better. I'll see you in the stairwell."

I did as I was told and joked around with the man at the front desk. Oddly enough his son had lost a suitcase when they had gone to London. He gave me a few pointers and I eagerly listened. Then he gave me the keys to room three twenty-one. It was the last room he had and it had a king-sized bed with two cots. I reluctantly paid the man even though there was no discount.

The little one would have to sleep with us. She hated cots every since her ordeal at summer camp.

Chapter sixteen

The room was quite a good one with a great view of the streets. It was exactly what we needed except for the beds. The cots were military. They'd be good for kids, but I wouldn't be able to sleep on it. Heidi had already picked a side.

"We can't…"

"Unless you want to sleep on the floor, you get the right side. We'll order room service and I'll answer. I'll need one of your shirts. I need to try and make myself look as frump as I can. Did you tell him I'd let myself go?"

"I said you don't stop talking."

"Fair enough. That would explain my black eyes."

"And little Jimmy doesn't eat seafood," I added. "Actually all the kids hate fish. We should probably stick with schnitzel. Who doesn't like pork?"

"Good job. I'll tell them you took our little imps to the park."

"Yes. Call them imps. That's what my wife would say."

"I got a call while I was waiting in the stairwell." She paused. "You really need to go back to Paris."

"I need to find my brother first."

"That's the thing. My buddy Jack thinks you might find him in Paris. Well, not Paris, but in that area. Georg Falkman was fostered by a family that moved him to Mainz when he was fourteen. When he was in his early twenties he moved to Saint Denis, just north of Paris. He fell off the radar shortly after."

"But he kept his name?"

"I would imagine, unless he was held up in a hotel room with an old flame, hiding out from her father who wanted to kill them."

"Are you trying to make a point here?"

"I'm thinking he's in Paris. Jack's looking through money trails, mortgages, car loans, overdue library books."

"So why is he a Falkman and me a Weisman?"

"It was a common practice. When he was given up he would have been given a new surname. It makes tracking him down almost impossible. A lot of kids want to find their birth parents, but if they were given up, there's a good chance that it was supposed to stay that way."

"Lucky for us." I pulled my phone out. "Should I call room service?"

"Only if you want my Dad to deliver." She grabbed my phone and started going through the menu.

"What are you doing?"

"Not that my father would figure this out, he's been in prison the last ten years, but phone GPS can be tracked if it's not turned off." She handed it back. "You're good now. Order it downstairs, face to face. Act panicked like you just lost three kids. Pay with cash and tell them your wife is in the room, and that you'll join me once you've rounded them up. Then get your ass back her as fast as you can."

"I'm not going to the park then?"

"I gotta get you out of this country. You're going to get yourself killed." She pushed me toward the door. "Four schnitzel dinners and one order of pancakes with extra syrup."

"Pancakes?"

"We have three kids, Jon. The chances of them all agreeing on schnitzel is like winning the lottery without buying a ticket. Besides, I want pancakes for breakfast."

"Right. We have kids. I think you're one of them." I opened the door, but stopped. "You are coming with me to Paris aren't you?"

"I don't know."

"Well you're sure as hell not staying here."

"It's not that easy, Jon."

"I get that. We just crawled through the walls of some butcher shop to get free from some gun-wielding psycho."

"That psycho was one of my right-hand men. His name is Slade."

"His name is Slade? Did you see a driver's license on that one?"

"Not the kind of guy you'd ask. He's a good man."

"Seriously? The guy just tore the door off a meat locker to get to us."

"With the return of my father, everything's complicated. My Dad automatically gets his role back. They follow him now."

"Are you saying this man was loyal to you before your Dad got out?"

"Him and about four hundred others. They all have a role. Some are mules, like we were, and others are muscle, recon, protection, eyes and distribution."

"Sounds like a company, except for the muscle."

"Don't kid yourself. Companies of any size have their own form of muscle. They call them lawyers. I called mine Slade."

"He's no longer loyal though."

"Like I said, it's complicated."

"I don't like complicated. Come with me to Paris."

"And that wouldn't be complicated?" She pulled me in and buried her face in my chest. "Where was this guy twelve years ago?"

"That guy was a coward. I never should have left you with him. What's worse, I never should have lost touch. I can't imagine what you've been through."

"You were young. It wasn't your job to take care of me." She opened the door and pushed me into the hallway. "Thanks for feeling bad about leaving me. That means a lot. Oh, and order a bottle wine. We're an old married couple, but only until the kids fall asleep. Then we can become party animals."

"And what if the children wake up?"

"Mommy's gonna lose her mind, flip out and start tossing her babies out the window."

"I hope they stay sleeping then. A reaction like that might ruin our vacation."

"I agree."

"You said four schnitzel, one pancake and two bottles of wine."

"Happy wife, happy life, and no ugly child splatter on the sidewalk."

"I won't forget the wine."

"I knew you were a catch."

Chapter seventeen

I woke up with Heidi wrapped around me. I'd cut a deal with her that we both remained dressed, and that we actually slept. Although we drank and talked until two in the morning, we were still dressed when the sun came up.

"Ready for pancakes."

One eye slowly opened. I expected it to squeak as if rust was holding it shut. "What time is it?"

"About eight."

"You're an early riser." The other eye opened and she rolled onto her back and tried to blink the night away. "Pancakes sounds good."

I got up and served her cold pancakes. I had one of the extra schnitzels. After breakfast we dressed and left the hotel for the train station. Heidi knew the airport would be crawling with her people. The train stations would too, but it would be easier to manoeuvre the crowds.

An hour and a half later, we had slipped onto one of the trains to Paris. Our talk from the night before continued in the dining car over a couple of strong black coffees. It actually went a lot faster than I thought as we rolled through the last few miles.

She looked out the window as the density of the rural houses grew. "So what am I going to do in Paris? It's not like I have anywhere to go, or know anybody, other than you, that is."

"Everybody's a stranger until you meet them."

She motioned putting a finger down her throat and barfing. "You have a way of making bleak look...uh, bleak."

"Whatever. Tell me more about Slade and the boys."

"What's to say? I was the Alpha and now I'm the hunted. I could change all that if I simply stand alongside my dad."

"Really?"

"I'd just have to rat you out."

I swallowed hard. "Can I buy you lunch? Maybe caviar, a good steak?"

"Don't worry. I'd never let him get you guys."

"Do you miss it?"

She looked up, scratched her head and nodded. "I do. I mean it's illegal and there's always someone trying to take your turf, but I handled it. I was damn good at it."

"How?"

"Befriending the police force didn't hurt, and keeping my shit out of the school system helped. The police were my muscle. When new players came to town I did my homework, gave them all the info and let them do the raids. It was good PR for them."

"But it wasn't the safest job, was it?"

"Stabbed three times, shot twice and once I was strangled until I passed out. That doesn't even cover the amount of black eyes or broken ribs. Occupational hazards. I'm a tough shit and now my boys were loyal to the end."

"Occupational hazards?"

"Sure. Cooks burn themselves, mechanics bang their knuckles when the wrench slips and postmen getting bit by dogs. It is what it is and nothing more."

"Mechanics don't get shot."

"I've also taken the Metro with over fifteen pounds of cocaine. Do you have any idea what the street value is on that?"

"Enough to buy a new house?"

"On the good side of the street, furnish it, and throw two new Jaguars in the driveway."

"Weren't you scared?"

"That's why I always took the big moves. It never even phased me. Fear and doubt are the signs you're carrying. Once, while I was carrying, I walked up to a police officer in Heilbronn and asked him what they were looking for. There were five of them nosing around a known drop spot. He told me to move it along."

"Brave."

"No, confident, and that confidence put me in charge after my father left. They'd follow me off a cliff if I asked them to."

"They're not lemmings."

"Wanna bet? They follow because that's what they do best. I lead because I suck at taking orders."

She wasn't lying. In all the years that we'd known each other, it was always her making the plans, organising the weekends. I thought we got caught up in her father's shit because we wanted money, but now I wonder. Could it be, she wanted her own team? Even back then, leading was in her blood. Her dad saw that and exploited it. They were quite the family. Now I understood why Eddy and Marcus had no use for her. Me, I was the dreamer. I thought I could change the world, and everyone in it.

"Did I lose you," she asked. "You seemed to be drifting."

"Just wondering where we left the kids." I smirked and took a sip of my coffee. "I actually have a proposition for you."

She leaned forward. "I'm listening."

"You're taking a big leap of faith, following me out to Paris. For that reason, I'm going to offer you my apartment, that's if you want."

The train pulled into the station and Heidi remained quiet. At least she was thinking about it. Why had I just offered that? It was more than I could handle. She was more than I could handle. Perhaps I could use her persuasive personality to help me find my brother.

"Come," Heidi said. "The train has stopped and we need to get off."

Still trying to tip the scale in favour of her staying at my apartment, I let her lead me through the station. We didn't hit the exit. Instead she pulled me four lanes over. She got up on her tippy-toes, hugged me and gave me a kiss. This one was passionate and yet respectful. Mouths remained closed. Then she pulled away, dropped back down and stepped onto the train.

"I love the fact that you're willing to let me stay with you when you're head's so messed up. You really are a great guy. The fact that you'd take me in after all the shit I put you through, like crawling through ducts and hiding in a crappy old hotels, it means a lot."

"It wasn't that bad."

"You don't get out much." She looked into my eyes and sighed. "I wish I would have followed you twelve years ago. Maybe we would have had three little imps for real, and a dog. I'd always wanted a dog."

"Guaranteed you wouldn't have been shot."

"With three kids there'd be no guarantees of that. Maybe some day, after the dust has settled, I'll look you up."

I stood stunned as the doors closed. The train started to roll and I looked up to see the destination was Frankfurt. What was this girl going back for?

Chapter eighteen

Paris, France

Back at my apartment I was restless. Heidi was halfway back to God only knew what. Her father would beat her bad for taking the money, even if she gave it back. She couldn't expect her people to be there for her anymore. Joseph was back and in obvious power. There was nothing good there, yet she was heading home.

I wasn't still thinking about Heidi while I went over Rebecca's things. I'd just done this with my parents and it had become surprisingly numbing. The clothing, the books, they were not my parents. They were just things, just like Rebecca's clothing and knick-knacks were just things. They weren't her and if anything, they just made me angry. Each item was a reminder of what had been ripped from my life.

I grabbed her jewellery box and threw it against the wall. It left a hole in the drywall before falling to the floor. I didn't care. I could fix that...or I could do something that Rebecca had always talked about. She had always dreamt of turning our apartment into one of those open concept places, knocking out walls and exposing a truer flow.

Hell. I could do that.

I took my foot and kicked it into the wall. A sledge hammer would have worked better but I didn't have one handy. I did have a claw hammer. With the help of that, and a few more sturdy kicks, the wall became an opening. Pictures fell to the floor and the mouldings split.

It felt good tearing that wall apart with my hands, therapeutic even. For that reason I went after another wall. Being in construction I knew which ones were load bearing. When I ran into wiring I took a saw and cut the joist away. Within an hour I had an open concept apartment. Wires hung freely. I'd have to do something about that, but not today. Today was all about the demo.

I sat on the coffee table and instantly regretted not putting drop cloths over the furniture. And how was Heidi doing? The train would have been rolling into the station about now. Surely she had a plan. So what was it? How could she make any of this right? She'd taken his money, helped me escape, and escorted me out of the country. He'd have to kill her.

Push the thought away, Jon. That isn't your problem. We all make choices. She was given the option to stay here. She could have stayed in his apartment. Maybe that was what scared her off. Maybe she knew it might shove us both down the rabbit hole, a hole where there'd be no escape. She knew I wasn't ready.

One of Rebecca's ornaments was teetering on the edge of the dresser. I must have bumped it when I was tearing out timbers. It was a cat I got her in Rüdesheim Germany. It was a weekend getaway and that was the first time she told me that she loved me. It had nothing to do with me buying her the porcelain cat or getting her drunk. She really did love me, said I was a great guy. Wasn't that what Heidi said?

I brushed the dust off the figurine with my thumb as I tried to push both women out of my mind. They were gone and I had a brother to find. I also had a mess to clean up. I'm thinking these renovations were a dumb idea.

There was a knock on the door and I made my way over the debris to the door. It was my neighbour, Old Lady Ester.

"Oh my. Is everything okay?"

"Sorry for the noise, Mrs Ester. Kind of a spur of the moment thing. I'm done making noise. I'll clean this up and keep it quiet."

She put a hand up to my cheek and brushed away a tear. I didn't even know it was there. Then she pursed her lips and gave me that sympathetic head tilt. I usually hated it when people did that, but this woman meant no harm. The woman was a widow. She'd felt my pain.

"If you need a place to stay, I have a guest room. I'd be happy to share it with you." She poked her head in the doorway. "You can't stay here anymore."

I looked back over my shoulder to see the broken drywall of two walls, twenty or more two by fours with nails sticking out of them, and dust. There was a lot of that. Wires were hanging and wood splinters covered the carpet.

"I'd be happy to have you."

It was a sweet gesture but like Heidi, I had a plan, albeit one I hadn't thought through. "Thank you for the offer, but I'll be okay."

"That's fine. If you change your mind or need anything at all, just ask."

"I will, and thank you."

I watched her leave, smiled when she entered her own apartment and closed the door. What was I thinking? I didn't have time for this right now. I had other jobs to finish, paying jobs. I needed to find a private detective, one that would do as good a job as my auburn-haired mother of three.

Oddly, I missed her. She was honest and helpful and as bad as she was at choosing friends and careers, there was a level of excitement that was a welcome distraction. It was the thing that attracted me to her, back when we were kids. She stood out as the one you wanted to hang out with. All the kids wanted to be her friend and yet she'd chosen Eddy, Marcus and myself.

I wish she'd have stayed in Paris. We'd be sharing beers and I'd have been dodging her corny advances. I wouldn't be wondering how I was going to get all this crap in the elevator.

The old lady was kind to check on me, and she was right about one thing, and that was that I couldn't stay here.

Under the rubble, I found my end table and a phone. I held it out and blew a puff of dust off of it. The cloud sailed toward the kitchen. Now the numbers could be seen.

I dialled Ingrid.

Chapter nineteen

I walked through the door of Ingrid's apartment with another box of my belongings. I set it down just outside the room that would be mine and then I headed straight for the kitchen. Something smelled real good.

When I entered the room, Marcus and Ingrid were sitting at the table eating. I quickly scooped up a plate full of food and joined them. "This looks really delicious."

Ingrid pointed to the candle. "Marcus and I thought you'd be by later."

"Ya. I did too." The potatoes were great. "The candle is a real nice touch."

Unlike Ingrid, Marcus didn't stop eating. "Try the roast. This girl can cook."

I tried it and he was right, she could. "This gravy is terrific. Hell, I may never leave."

At that point Ingrid dropped her fork, got up and left the table. She returned with a full glass of wine.

"Is everything okay?" I asked her.

"Wonderful."

She didn't look wonderful. I forced a smile. She didn't. "Was I interrupting something? I mean I didn't see a necktie on the door handle."

"I don't own one."

Marcus tapped my plate with his fork. "Try the carrots. Cooked perfectly."

70

He looked over to Ingrid and I caught him shooting her a wink. It was the kind that told her to cut me some slack. "That was crazy seeing Eddy and Heidi."

"Eddy lives around here somewhere."

"Really? How do you know that?"

"I flew back with him a couple days ago."

That caught Ingrid off guard. "You were in town?"

"I came back just for the day. I wanted to go see Rebecca."

She reached over and put her hand on mine. "You were the one who fixed the grass, weren't you?"

"It looked like a jigsaw puzzle gone wrong. I just needed to make it real."

"Have you called her parents yet?"

"No, I'm practising. I've picked up the phone a dozen times."

Marcus understood. He wanted to know more about our two church crashers. "You see Heidi again?"

"A few times."

"Didn't I tell you to run if you saw her?"

"Who's Heidi? Was she that girl at the house, the one with the dark hair?" Ingrid asked.

Marcus hushed her. "What does she want?"

Ingrid persisted. "What's going on here?"

I hesitated. There was no easy way to say this. "Joseph is out."

Ingrid kept the questions coming. "Who's Joseph?"

Marcus stopped eating, dropped his cutlery down and exhaled as if he didn't want to inhale. He did anyway. "Joseph is a guy that was supposed to rot in jail. He's out?"

"Heidi showed up at my parent's place shortly after you called. She had a black eye. He gave it to her."

"He wanted us too?"

"Me, more than anything."

"Is Joseph a boyfriend?" Ingrid was getting impatient.

"Her father." I explained their odd relationship, the violence and the fact that he was angry that I hadn't taken the fall for him. I reluctantly told them both about the meat locker, the train ride and the fact that Heidi had gone back. There was no mention of the hotel, the three kids or the kiss.

"So let me see if I've got this straight." Ingrid put her glass down. "You three used to work for her father moving drugs?"

"We were mules," Marcus corrected. "We just handled packages. He never told us what he was moving. We often assumed, never asked and always got paid. When he went to jail we all scattered."

"All but Heidi. She told me she took over the business," I added.

"She's a drug dealer?"

"No, Ingrid." It bothered me to hear her called that. "She took over to keep that shit out of the schools."

"Oh, she's a nice drug dealer."

"I guess." I realised how dumb it all sounded. "Doesn't matter. Her father is out and back in charge."

"Why do you think she went back?"

"It's all she knows. While he was gone she ran it as good, if not better, than he did. She dealt with the competition, kept her guys loyal and clients satisfied."

Ingrid shook her head. "Sounds like you admire her."

"Respect. If you knew where she came from, you would too. The girl's a strong one. That being said I'm worried about her."

Marcus put a hand on my shoulder. "I get that you're worried, but trust me, you have to let it go. This isn't the same girl you knew. Back in the day you had a boyfriend's influence, but the years have changed that."

"You used to date her?" Ingrid asked.

I automatically went on the defensive. "Twelve years ago. We were teenagers."

"Did you love her?"

I wanted to lie. Marcus wanted me to lie. I could see it in his eyes. "Of course I did. Heidi is a good person. It's her father that's the monster. Tell her, Marcus."

Marcus's eyes had given up on me. "She's also a monster, Jon. Don't kid yourself. She ran her father's business like a pro. A sweet person couldn't do that. I know none of us could."

"I'm not a businessman," I said in her defence.

"You know what I mean. To do that job, she'd have to have people beat up or worse. Lord knows her father never hesitated. I think he enjoyed it."

"Well she doesn't."

This time it was Ingrid winking at Marcus to back him off. She could tell I was on the defensive and there'd be no winning. "How about we cool this off with dessert?"

I quickly finished my plate while Ingrid ran off to the fridge. Marcus stared at me, no doubt biting down hard on his lip. He had no use for Heidi and I got that. He never saw the side of her that I saw. With me she was playful. With them she was calculating. Was she playing me? It wouldn't matter now. I was here and she was back in Germany.

Ingrid dropped three plates down. Each one had a slice of cheesecake with fresh strawberries and whipped cream. It tasted amazing and as Ingrid ate hers, I noticed the split down the centre. She tried to hide it with berries and cream.

"This was a dinner for two, wasn't it?"

Marcus nodded.

Ingrid giggled. "Marcus and I just took our relationship to the next level."

"Seriously!" I looked to Marcus. "You mean you..."

"Yep." He held up a piece of paper. "I made her an equal partner in my modelling company."

It was a big step for him, but not at all what I was thinking. "That's wonderful."

Chapter twenty

T he next morning I awoke to the smell of coffee. I quickly got dressed, brushed my teeth and made my way out into Ingrid's world. There was no breakfast in this world, but that was okay. I could pick something up later.

"Hey. I'm sorry about last night. I never knew you guys were doing a date night."

"That's fair. I'm telling you now that we're trying again tonight, so you'll have to find your own supper. Is that okay?"

"I'll grab something at the deli by my place. I have a busy day ahead of me. I have to see my private investigator and clean up the mess at my place."

"Why'd you trash the place?"

"Rebecca had always wanted to open it up. Seemed like a good idea at the time."

"Next time you're missing her, do what the rest of us do and go get drunk. It's a proven cure."

"What if I get drunk and end up somewhere I shouldn't be?"

"I hate to say it, Jon, but that's part of the healing process."

"What?"

"I loved Rebecca. She was an amazing girl and you'll never find another like her. The next best thing is a good glass of wine and distraction."

"That's terrible advice."

"I know. I miss her too and wine is the only thing holding me together."

"That and your new business partner."

"That's my distraction." She pointed to her signature on the contract. "I think I want to mess with him. I have the power now."

"I wouldn't."

"Just something small like trying to change the Company name."

"That's small? I wouldn't. Marcus doesn't have a French sense of humour. He would lose his mind."

"He would, wouldn't he?" Her humour wasn't French. It was more satanic.

I finished my coffee and made my way to the bathroom. I needed a shave. I also needed to put on a better shirt and comb my hair.

When I was ready to head out I heard her at the door talking to somebody through the intercom. That was my cue to get out of her way. "Well I'll be going now."

"Okay."

I found my coat on the back of a chair and headed for the door. As I did I heard a light knocking.

Ingrid didn't walk me out, but heard the knock. "Can you get that, Jon?"

"Okay." I opened the door to see my Rebecca standing there. She was alive. I just stared. I'm sure my mouth was slightly open.

From the kitchen Ingrid called out, "*Qu'est-ce*, Johannes?"

When I didn't say anything, the woman at the door answered. "It's me, Madeline. I brought the marble monster."

This wasn't Rebecca. This was her identical looking sister. With that I broke my silence. "I'm so sorry, Madeline. You look so much like her. I…"

"Rebecca and Madeline were twins Johannes," Ingrid reminded me.

"I know that." I shook my head and stepped back. "Please, come in."

Ingrid gave me a shove toward the doorway. "You are going to be late if you don't get moving."

"Yes, I uh, it was nice to see you, Madeline." I stepped through the doorway, stopped, and turned back to her. I wanted to say something, but closed my mouth and walked away. I couldn't say anything that wouldn't make me sound foolish, desperate, or crazy. She was my Rebecca, except for the beige pants suit, the small boy and the fact she didn't seem to recognise me.

My heart was beating in my chest as I walked down the hallway and my dazed stupidity lingered like a bad smell. It followed me out to my car and caused me to run a stop sign. Thankfully the roads were quiet. I'd only ever seen Madeline a couple times. Once was at her father's birthday. It was a short visit. They came, had a drink and left. I could see right away that Lawrence had little use for them. I'm not sure why, they seemed like lovely people. I'm sure he had his reasons.

My stomach churned. It was hard to see her, and even harder to believe it wasn't my Rebecca. It was obvious that she didn't feel the same. She saw me as that guy she'd maybe met twice, but I'd left no memorable impression. Maybe Rebecca had talked to her about me, but the two of us had never really spoken except to comment on the weather or her mother's cooking.

I had to pull over. There was a back alley that beckoned me so I pulled over, opened the driver's door and left the contents of my stomach there. Wiping my mouth on my sleeve, I closed the door and quickly sped off.

Was it fair that Rebecca had a twin? I found it border line cruel. How was I supposed to get over losing the woman if I was reminded of her every time I saw her sister? Normally this wouldn't have been a problem, but if we both hang around with Ingrid, how I was supposed to move on. Maybe I did need Heidi to help me with this. It wasn't like she'd say no.

What was I thinking? I didn't want to get over Rebecca. I wanted to hurt. I wanted to miss her. I wanted to be mad at her for leaving me like this. I just didn't need her sister throwing my emotions around like rice at a wedding. What was I saying? I couldn't blame her for being a twin. I could, however, talk to Ingrid. I don't want to be an ass, but she had to know how this would affect me.

Maybe I needed to talk to her, tell her she couldn't have her for a friend. There were seven billion other people on the planet. She needed to pick one of them instead.

I'd call her in a couple hours. Surely she'd be okay with that.

Chapter twenty one

I don't think I gauged Ingrid's reaction accurately. It made me wonder if I caught her at a bad time as I pulled into the parking lot of what looked like a rather nice hotel. The carpet was red, well travelled and quite cushiony under foot. The front desk was manned by a young woman who obviously wished she were anywhere but behind that desk.

She didn't look up, but heard me coming. "Good morning, Sir. Can I help you?"

"Unless you have a major in psychology, all you can do is give me a room."

She lifted her head in confusion. "I'm sorry?"

"Uh, how much for a room?"

She under-enthusiastically pushed a pamphlet with the different rates in front of me. This was not a girl for small talk. I wanted to tell her that my wife and three children would be joining us, but this woman, not realising it was an inside joke, would have likely charged me extra.

And what was that wife of mine doing? Was she running a pound of cocaine up to some downtown club, or lying in a ditch bleeding. If nothing else, Heidi was an interesting girl. It wasn't like I missed having her around, although I couldn't really say I didn't. She reminded me of Halloween candy. Reaching inside your pillowcase you could find chocolate bars, those rocket candies and those mini packets of gum. You could also grab a handful of crushed cookies, unwrapped toffees and broken suckers. Every handful was different and every day with Heidi was unlike any other.

As the morning morphed into afternoon, I walked into my room and did not throw a suitcase on the bed. My stuff was all at Ingrid's place. I'd swing by and pick it up later, or tomorrow. For now, a welcome distraction was eating away at me. I picked up the phone and dialled Heidi hoping for a chocolate bar and not a handful of those crushed cookies.

She answered on the first ring. "My Darling. How are you? How are the kids?"

I smiled at getting the chocolate bar. "I thought they were with you?"

"Oops. I sold somebody's children earlier for bus money. I hope they weren't ours."

"Selling children for bus money. I've heard about that. It's not a thing here in Paris, but I've heard Germany is big on it."

"That and we drink maple syrup out of cowboy boots."

"Now I know you're messing with me. That's a Canadian thing."

"You got me. What's up with the dingle? I never thought I'd hear from you again."

"I don't know. I'm just a worrywart." I cleared my throat. "Have you seen your father?"

There was almost a full minute of silence before she answered. That meant it was bad. "I saw him last night."

"How are you doing?"

"You remember how it goes, fat lips, and broken teeth. I think he likes to mess me up like this so that he can parade me in front of the others. Only a savage would hurt his daughter like this, so don't mess with him. Little do they know that I'm no more family to him than they are."

"But you're his daughter."

"No. He's my boss. If he were my father, I'd get Christmas presents and a cake for my birthday. Do you know what I got for my last birthday?"

I thought hard for a second. "Oh my God. Happy belated Birthday. It was yesterday wasn't it?"

"Now you know what I got for my birthday."

"I wish I was there to get you something. You deserve better than that."

"My prince. What would you have bought me?"

"Oh I don't know. It would be something nice, something to make you feel pretty. Maybe I'd buy you a…"

"A new vacuum so that I could clean up after our kids? Don't bother. I sold them for bus money, remember?"

"No, damn it. I mean like flowers and some nice perfume."

"Whoa, Prince Charming. Don't get pissed off at me."

"I'm not mad at you. I'm pissed off at your father. I'd like to come down there and…"

"And what, kick the shit out of him. Maybe he'd start treating me like a daughter? Maybe I'd get a stuffed unicorn for my next birthday? Listen and listen close, Jon. If you come here he will hurt you, and I don't mean a split lip. He'll break ribs, knees and maybe your back. You can't handle him, but I can."

"I'm not afraid of dying." Which was a stupid thing to say. I was definitely afraid.

"Oh, he won't kill you," she laughed. "You'd be lucky if he slipped up and killed you. He'd want you to be crippled up, like a billboard of suffering. He'd put you in a wheelchair so that you could spend the rest of your life thinking about him. Every time you dragged yourself out of bed, banging knuckles on walls while you wheeled around your apartment, you'd think of him."

"Come back to Paris. Get away from him, before he hurts you like that."

"We're good now. I know my place."

"Your place is Paris."

"Really, Jon? You going to put a ring on my finger?" She knew how to shut me up.

Back in the day I was ready to put a ring on that finger. We were young, and we were in love. If it weren't for Rebecca, I would go out and buy her that jewellery. Once again, Heidi found herself grasping for the short straw.

"That's what I thought. I know you still love her and my name isn't Charity."

"I'm worried about you."

"That's okay. I worry about me too, but this is real life. We play the cards we're dealt and I'm not so bad at this game. Have a little more faith in me."

"Maybe I shouldn't have called."

"Are you kidding? I got a Happy Birthday from you. I couldn't have asked for a better gift. Screw the diamonds and gold, and I'm being serious, not sarcastic. It was good to hear from you. Oh, and if you ever call again, I'll block your number. Forget about me, Jon. It's for the better."

"You know I still care for you."

"And I love you for it. Now go take care of the kids and don't let little Jimmy play with the cat in the bathtub. It never ends well."

The call ended and I could feel my chest tighten.

Chapter twenty two

C ollecting my thoughts, I tossed them in a box marked Hard Knocks. Why I'd had such horrendous luck with women, I don't know. I did know, however, that I needed some fresh air and maybe a drink. I'd seen a pub a half block down the street and it would serve my mood well.

"Jon." It was Fast Eddy Cruiser standing by a news kiosk. He'd just bought a newspaper.

"Hey Eddy. How are you doing?"

"I'm good, and yourself?"

"Feeling awfully sorry for myself. I was just about to hit that pub for lunch. Do you want to join me?"

"I'll do one better. I'll buy the first beer."

We made our way into the bar and found a table in the corner. Old habits die hard. The waitress caught Eddy's eye when she came right over. She was petite with a full head of blonde hair. I knew from Marcus and his models that most of that hair wasn't hers, but Eddy didn't. His eyes were locked.

I ordered and paid while Eddy tried every pickup line he knew. None of them worked, although I think she was quite flattered by his resilience.

"So what's on your mind?" he asked. "Talk to me."

I shrugged. "It's a little of everything. I pissed off Marcus's girlfriend, saw Madeline, and just got off the phone with Heidi. It's a lot to deal with."

"You talked to Heidi? Did she call you?"

"I called her."

"Why? Hasn't she done enough to you?"

None of them got her like I did. "She's not her father. She's…"

"The one that's going to get you killed. Stay away from her, Jon. Promise me."

"You sound like Marcus. He can't stand her either."

"Trust your friends." He took a drink. "We remember it all a little different than you do. She's a trouble-making opportunist."

"She's broken. I'll admit that, but she's not malicious."

"And our waitress is into me, so much that I had to ask her to leave me alone."

I laughed. "The poor woman ran for her life. You need new pickup lines."

"And you need to tell me who this Madeline chick is."

"She Rebecca's twin sister, and I'm talking identical." I downed half my beer after spitting that out.

"Ouch. That had to be hard."

"I froze, stared, and acted like quite the idiot. It was like I expected her to look at me the way Rebecca used to. I just wanted her to be glad to see me, but she wasn't. That being said, she'd only met me a couple of times. What did I expect?"

"You wanted her to be Rebecca. There's no crime in that. I'd be just as messed up if that happened to me. Don't beat yourself up over it, and as for Ingrid, if she's a friend then she'll understand."

"Thanks. I know you're right. I just can't get Heidi out of my mind. I should be thinking about Rebecca and my parents."

"Hold it. I didn't know there were rules to grieving. I think you get to feel what you feel and as for Heidi, you two were inseparable for years. I get why you're thinking about her. She looks better than ever and she has a very strong personality. I see the attraction. Here's the thing. You're a nice guy and have always been attracted to helping others. The more they need you, the more you love them. I never met Rebecca, but I'd bet you she was a little broken and that was what you saw in her."

"Nah, it was her eyes."

"Liar. Nobody notices the eyes first."

I gave a guilty head nod. Rebecca was attractive in so many ways. It wasn't until I really got to know her that I noticed the purity in her eyes. It was like looking into the eyes of a small child the night before Christmas.

"The eyes are what I remember most."

"She sounds like she was a wonderful woman."

I could only smile.

"So did you get all that stuff taken care of with your parents? I know you were thinking of listing the house. Did you do that?"

"I did."

"I'll make a call later. I might know someone who's interested in it. I knew this couple from way back and ran into them shortly after seeing you guys. They just moved to Frankfurt and need a place. They couldn't afford anything too inner city, but your parent's place could work."

"I priced it low for a quick sale, so talk to them. Tell them it's got a new roof and the plumbing was overhauled about five years ago. It's a solid house."

"Right on. Even if it did need a little work, I'd be happy to help them."

"Do you do renovations?"

"I do…" He paused. "I think I need to show you what I do. Have you got a minute?"

"I have things to do, but none of it is pressing. I think I'm in need of a day off. Is it a project?"

"It is."

He picked up his beer and started to pour it down his throat in several large gulps. I did the same. We'd talked about getting a bite to eat, but that could wait. Talking to Eddy pulled me out of my pity-party.

"Do you like popcorn?"

"For lunch?"

He laughed, put the beer down and started for the door. I almost finished my beer, took it with me as far as I could and set it on a table by the front door. Eddy started up the sidewalk and I tried to keep his pace. He was excited in a way that I'd never seen before.

Eddy had always been a shadow. Marcus and I even called him that from time to time, but never to his face. As a shadow, he never had an opinion, never demanded anything from us, and he never made the call. When I think about it, it was Heidi always making the decisions and arranging the fun and misadventures. To her we were all shadows. Eddy was the darkest.

He stopped in front of an old movie theatre. It had been closed for years. There was a sign up on the marquee lights and it read *Opening Soon*.

Chapter twenty three

Pulling out a ring of keys, Eddy found the one for the front door and unlocked it. We walked in and the smell of paint and fresh carpet made me grin. He walked over to the electrical boxes and flipped on the lights. It was beautiful.

The carpet was new and the walls boasted a fresh coat of paint. The brass door handles and fixtures were tarnished. He'd left them to give the place an aged feel and it worked. The theme was an obvious a fifties and sixties one. I took a few steps toward the actual theatre part, where the screens and seats were, when the posters stopped me. Talk about nostalgic.

The first poster was the great *Phantom of the Opera*. It was the 1943 poster with Susanna Foster and Claude Rains, a classic. The one beside it was *La Vie en Rose*. There was *Last Tango in Paris*, a Bernardo Bertolucci flick with Marlon Brando, and *Belle de Jour* with Catherine Deneuve. My favourite poster was *Moulin Rouge*.

"Wow. These are breathtaking, Eddy."

"I'm glad you like them. I have a few others and will rotate them from week to week when I open."

"When you open?"

"Yes, Jon. This place was a dump and I got it for a steal. I've put three years into it and finally have it where I want it. I'm going to open it in a couple weeks. Nothing but the older stuff too. Marilyn will start us off with *Gentlemen Prefer Blondes*."

"Because you are a gentleman."

"Always loved Marilyn. I wanted to start with *Seven Year Itch*, but this is Opening Night for me and I know the other was more popular. Hopefully I can scratch a living at it and hang up my tool belt."

"Well you'll have my business. Have you got staff and everything picked out?"

"I'm in the process. I'm looking for women our age that want a few extra dollars. I'd rather not hire kids. I remember how hard it was being one. We'd rather be talking to each other than working. I want this theatre to make the customer important again. I'm sick of going out and being ignored by waitresses and shop clerks."

I thought of the woman at the front desk of the hotel where I was staying. "I think that's a great idea. I can't wait."

"I like your enthusiasm. Can I get you to spread the word for me? I'm going to be putting up posters on telephone poles and such, but nothing beats word of mouth."

"I'll definitely help you out."

"And opening night means free popcorn."

He motioned to the big popcorn machine. It looked like something you'd find at a circus. Then he opened the doors to the theatre. The rows and rows of old seats were all freshly recovered. Walking through the doors was like entering some time warp. I felt I was walking into a theatre from the fifties. I had to flip one of the seats down and take a seat.

It sucked me in and I stared at the red curtain as if it would actually open for me. The lights would dim and the countdown would start. Then the movie would start. Maybe Eddy would start the movie with an old French cartoon, something short, but able to pull a laugh or two out of the crowd.

"This is fantastic."

"It means a lot to me that you like it, Jon. I wanted you to know that I'd done something with my life after we all went our separate ways."

"I didn't doubt you would. You were always the quiet one, but you were also the observant one. You said we needed to get out of the drug courier business long before any of the rest of us did. I was enamoured with the money."

"No. You were giddy with the girl that you were working with. She loved the danger and you loved her. You'd still be doing it if it weren't for Joseph's arrest. That night changed everything."

I didn't remember much of that night except for Joseph threatening me if I didn't tell them who the drugs belonged to. I was expected to take the rap and when I hesitated, he flipped out. I looked to Heidi for a sign, but she was being hauled off kicking and screaming.

"Two weeks. That's exciting."

"It is. It's also been a money pit. I hope I can recoup some of it."

"Are you okay for money?"

"Not to worry. I'm good, and you can never lose on real-estate."

"I'm just saying, I've come into an inheritance. I'd love to invest."

"Hold onto your money, Jon. I know how you love a cause, but I'm not it. I'm doing okay and most of this has been pay as I go."

"Well I'll be here opening night and I'll bring Marcus and Ingrid. I owe them for screwing up a date night. They'd love it."

"Great."

"But I need to go." I wanted to get into my story, private investigators and a long lost brother, but decided to let him have his day. This was quite the accomplishment.

He walked me out and gave me a clap on the back. "Things will get better, Jon. You're a good person and you'll be fine."

"Especially if I'm eating free popcorn." I gave a wave and started back for the hotel. Maybe I could work on the apartment today. When the phone in my pocket buzzed I pulled it out. I had a text.

It was from Heidi and it read

P/U Airport tomorrow night?
Flight arrives 11pm

I typed quickly which for me was pretty slow. She had changed her mind and that was okay with me. I thought of taking her to a movie and let the guilt wash the thought away.

See you then :)
Kids look forward to seeing you

She responded.

Same :)

Chapter twenty four

Morning in my new hotel room felt right. There were no reminders of Rebecca anywhere I looked, no Ingrid and Marcus trying to move their relationship to any next levels. I wasn't dragging a wife or three kids through the streets of Frankfurt and there was no mess of drywall dust or lumber. Because of this, I had actually slept in, but now I was awake and I needed a coffee.

The same girl was working at the front desk. She gave me a double take and it was flattering until I realised I was wearing the same clothes from yesterday. It was time to make a trip to Ingrid's place for my stuff. I left right away.

The door at Ingrid's was slightly ajar so I just walked in. The woman was standing there looking as lovely as ever. I had to catch myself. This wasn't Rebecca. "Madeline?"

She turned to see me standing there. "Hi."

I walked over, studying her in a way that wouldn't be too obvious. The eyes, the nose, the lips, she really was identical. "You look great."

"Pardon me?"

The comment wasn't a terrible thing under normal circumstances, but considering the fact I was looking at her like she was her sister, it wasn't good. I tried to shake my gaze.

It was time for me to relax, be cool. "It's good to see you."

"Same."

She politely walked over to me and held out her hand. I think that meant for me to take it and give it a shake. I did and her skin was deliciously soft. I had to remind myself to let her have her hand back.

That was when I noticed something on her wrist and pulled it forward. "What happened to you?"

"What's…?" She followed my eyes to her wrist.

There was a ring of blue and green around it. "How'd you get that bruise?"

"I uh…"

Ingrid quickly came to her rescue. "She was changing a light bulb and fell off a stool. She was lucky she didn't break anything."

She pulled her hand back and rubbed the bruise. "Yes, stupid stool, shot out like it had a mind of its own."

"Next time call me. I'd be happy to come over and help." I meant that as a friendly gesture, but I'm sure it came out wrong. I was trying too hard. I looked over to Ingrid and she was feeling the same.

Ingrid stepped between us. "How about I walk you to your car."

She was talking to Madeline who was leaving, but I wasn't ready to let her go. "You don't have to leave, do you?" I regretted saying it the second it came out.

"I do." She took her son's hand. "Thank you, Ingrid. You want to come down and see my new wheels?"

"Yes."

Madeline turned back to me when she reached the door. "It was nice to see you again."

I nodded, knowing that she didn't mean it. I'd said too many stupid things. I honestly don't remember ever acting this weird. Granted I was never the coolest guy in the room, but I was never an idiot like this either.

I packed up my clothes, dropped by my apartment to get a few more items and left everything at the hotel. I'd even grabbed a few of Madeline's… I mean Rebecca's things. I still needed to torture myself with them.

Driving down Rue de Malte, I realised I was lost. Not lost like I wasn't sure where I was, but lost like what was I doing? Did I want to get to work on the apartment, head back to Ingrid's in hopes of resting my eyes on her newest friend, or just drive around until I ran out of gas? The latter would be coming up soon if I didn't figure it out.

The decision was made as I pulled into the parking lot of my private investigator. He was a younger guy and eager to get work. Not being a seasoned investigator, I knew he would make up for his inexperience with enthusiasm.

He sat behind an older desk, one likely given away when they were renovating the office building across the street. He got up when I entered the room. "Morning, Mr Weisman."

"Good morning, and it's Jon." I didn't have the heart to tell him it was now afternoon. "How are you making out?"

"This is a tough one, but I took the information you gave me and ran it through the system. I didn't find much, but there was one thing that makes me think you were right about him being in the area.

A little over a year ago there was a report done at the Clinique des Franciscaines. A man bearing the name Georg Falkman was brought in with a nasty cut to his lower right leg. He received eighteen stitches. The accident was a work one so I should be able to go through government agencies and see if there were any disability or lost wages paid out."

"That sounds good."

"If we're lucky we can get an address as to where these payments were made."

"What are we waiting for?"

"Well, a lot of these agencies require paper requests. They've already been sent out. I imagine a week is a good estimate before we hear anything. I hope that is okay."

"I've gone a lifetime without him. What's another week?"

"I've also found out that the man is thirty-two years old. He was born on January first."

"A New Years Baby?"

"No. A John Doe Baby. It was common to change the birth date. Again it was to keep the child from being found."

"Poor guy entered the world a complete unknown."

"That's why most of them grow up in trouble. I'm also running his name through the police records. I'm hoping I don't find anything there."

"Same."

"Just like I hope we don't find him when I get the request back for Death Certificates."

"I've run his name through the phone system and he's either not in the system or doesn't want to be in the system. Hopefully we get more when those government records arrive in a week."

I got up to leave, extended my hand and let him shake it. He was a good man and seemed like he was on the right track. "Thank you. I'll swing by in a week if I don't hear from you sooner."

For now I had to get back to Ingrid's place. Maybe Madeline would be there.

Chapter twenty five

I left the office, started my car and headed back to Ingrid's apartment. Not only did I have news about my brother, but I wanted to apologise for the way I'd been acting. Madeline was dropping her off when I pulled up. Badly, I wanted to get out of my car and play the part of the idiot. Instead I waited until she left.

Ingrid was surprised to see me. "What is happening to you, Jon?"

"She looks just like her. Even her eyes look like her. How the hell am I not supposed to act the fool?"

"Uh, realise that she is not her. I only say that because she is going through a lot. Imagine waking up to a whole new life. She has a husband, a child and can't remember her sister. She's so worried about it all that she's getting sick."

"What was up with her wrist?"

"I don't know. She's having me over for supper tonight and I'm going to check the guy out."

"What if he's abusive?"

"Don't jump to conclusions, Jon. But if he is, I'll have to be her friend, help her make the right decision."

"Can I come?"

"What? No. You act all weird around her. You act like that in front of her husband and you'll get beat up."

"I'm not afraid of him."

"Him? I'll be the one beating you up. She doesn't need your bewildered staring."

"I won't stare. I won't say anything stupid. In fact, I won't even talk. I'll just be the perfect house guest."

"Jon, why don't you just..."

"Come on, Ingrid."

"If you go, you cannot bring up Rebecca. She doesn't even remember her. You cannot bring up how she looks, smells, or how good she cooks. No compliments. You cannot stare, drool or stand there with your mouth partially open."

"I got it."

"I don't think you have."

"Look, Madeline is my sister-in-law and Nicolas is my nephew. I don't have a lot of family. I need this, Ingrid."

I could tell she was thinking about it, and I was right. Other than a few aunts and uncles, I was alone. Sure I had a few friends, but even that was an issue.

"Okay."

"Thank you, Ingrid. I promise I'll be good."

"She's your sister-in-law. Just remember that."

"I will."

"Besides, I want to see how he reacts around other strong men."

"What?"

"Does he get the whole testosterone thing going, puffing out his chest and bossing his wife around?"

"I'll kill him..."

"No you won't," she snapped. "I want to see how this guy acts. I also need to be her friend. You freak out and we'll both be banned from her life and from their home. She might need us so don't screw this up."

As usual I was speaking before my brain could catch up. Ingrid was right. Madeline needed a friend and I was only there to flush out reactions. I could do that and hold my temper. I had to. "That's what I was thinking."

"I know." She patted my back. "Such a big lug. I'm sorry you've been through so much, Jon. It will get better. And if you want, you can stay here. I didn't mean to push you out. Sometimes I forget how hard it's been for you."

"Actually, I like my hotel room. They make a better cup of coffee."

That was when her hands landed on me and she started to shove me in the direction of the door. "Out. My coffee is good. You wouldn't know a good cup of coffee if it…"

"That mud, a good cup of coffee? I'm going to get going now. I have a dinner to get ready for."

She continued to shove me. "*Mon café est le meilleur. Vous êtes un fou sans goût…*"

I got the door open just in time. "Ya, ya. Should I pick you up at six?"

"*Qui. Merci. Les hommes sont des garçons et sont un…*"

I closed the door behind me and basked in the silence as I made my way to my car. She'd have to get over the fact that her coffee wasn't the best. Maybe it would even push her to get it right, not that it was all that bad. I'd just had better and she was fun to tease.

I returned to her apartment four hours later. A cup of coffee was stuffed in my face. "Drink."

I had a sip and decided to lie through my teeth before I lost them. "Now that's a cup of coffee. Really amazing."

She took it from me, poured it down the sink and reached for her coat.

"Now let's go meet Madeline's husband. You look good by the way."

I watched her leave the apartment as if she had not a care in the world. On the drive she was chatty and politely went over the role I needed to play. It wasn't like we wanted this man to be an asshole, preferred he wasn't, but we needed to know.

I just sat behind the steering wheel and drove while she talked. The whole way over there one question kept rolling around in my head. Did all women have split personalities?

I never asked it.

Chapter twenty six

The drive over to Madeline's house was a short one. Nicolas was dressed in his Sunday best and greeted us at the door. As her shadow, Ingrid entered first and I stayed in the background. I'd brought a gift. Nicolas's eyes were like saucers as he ran the package over to the table where he carefully began opening it.

The gift was a book of fairy tales, complete with pictures and a leather cover. Behind me I heard Lawrence mutter something.

"What do you say, Nicolas?" Madeline asked.

"*Merci.*" He held it up to her. "What, Mom?"

"It's some new bedtime tales, Nicolas. I'll read you one tonight." He hugged the book as if it were a favourite teddy bear.

"Thanks Johannes," she said. "That was very nice of you."

"Please, call me Jon." Jon was what she'd preferred to call me. She said Johannes was something a parent might call a child when they were in trouble.

She let her eyes linger on me and I didn't mind. It was like she was warming up to me. Did that mean I was trying too hard? Hopefully her husband didn't make too much out of the 'Jon' comment.

She stepped beside her husband for a formal introduction. "Lawrence, this is my friend Ingrid and her friend Jon Weisman."

He extended his arm and I shook it. Ingrid stayed a step back.

Madeline broke what had become an awkward silence. "I hope you all like lasagne. Why don't you all take a seat while I put the garlic bread in the oven?"

Lawrence held his drink with the same hand that he held his cigar. He took a sip and held it in his mouth for a second before swallowing. "What do you do in Paris, Jon?"

"I'm a contractor, although I've taken a break to go on a quest."

"A quest?"

"Yes. I recently got some interesting news. My parents died a month ago and, in the will, they mentioned a brother. I'm taking some time off to go look for him."

"Really?" Lawrence failed miserably at acting interested in what I had to say. Instead he turned to the bar. "Want a drink?"

"That would be great."

Madeline returned with the bread and we all took our places at the table. Lawrence, not being shy, scooped the largest piece to his plate. The rest of us also dished up while Madeline cut Nicolas's meal up into smaller pieces. He puckered up and started to blow on them like there were birthday candles. It looked cute.

I took a bite and wiped my mouth with the napkin. "This is delicious, Madeline."

"Thanks Johannes."

My compliment hung in the room like a bad smell. I think Madeline would have preferred I said nothing. We all felt the uneasiness and Ingrid took note. This was what we were looking for.

"Jon is looking for a brother, Madeline," Lawrence told her. He wanted to move the evening along. Eat, talk, and then everybody could get the hell out his house. "What happens if you find him?"

"Well, I'd hope to get to know him. But I also want to share our inheritance with him." I shrugged. "It's more than I need, and you never know, this guy might need a break. Maybe he's not doing so well."

Lawrence stopped chewing. "Are you serious?"

"Of course. He's my brother."

"This guy got a name?"

"Yes, and it's being run through government records. We're running it through adoption agencies, the National, Sister Mary and the Mac Noble."

"Mac Noble?" This sparked Lawrence's interest. "I didn't realise that agency was still around?"

His knowing of this place caught us all off guard.

"You've heard of them?" Madeline asked.

"Mac Noble was the agency that handled my adoption."

"Oh, right. I must have forgotten, with the accident and all."

This could only be a blessing. Maybe he could help me find my brother. If anybody could get things done it was somebody who had been there.

Lawrence turned back to me. "So what name are we working with? Weisman?"

I put my fork down and let hope widen my eyes. "I can give you the name, but he wasn't born here, or in Frankfurt. I think he was born in Koblenz. And he's not a Weisman. He's a Falkman."

Lawrence traded the fork in his hand for his drink. He knew something. "Falkman?"

"Yes, Georg Falkman."

"Really?" Lawrence pushed his half-eaten plate of food away as he slumped back in his chair.

He knew something. His thoughts, now in overload, could only mean that he knew this Georg guy. The man didn't bother to hide the fact that he was shaken.

"Are you okay?" Madeline asked. Whatever this was, it was big. "Do you know that name, Lawrence?"

"Oh, I know this Georg guy alright." He held his drink in front of him, mesmerised by the sound of the cubes clinking against the edge of the glass.

We all sat dazed by his reaction.

I leaned forward needing an answer. "How do you know him, Mr Trembley?"

Lawrence downed his glass of scotch. It seemed to bring him back to us. "Georg Falkman was my name before I was adopted."

Chapter twenty seven

Ingrid cleared the dishes while Lawrence and I retired to the study. We needed to catch up. I could see Madeline watching us from the doorway of the kitchen. In a weird kind of way I felt closer to her in all the right ways. She was my sister, and not because she was Rebecca's sister, but because Lawrence was my brother.

I took a seat in the chair in front of his desk. He freshened my drink, lit a cigar for me and handed it over. "These are Cubans, best money can buy. This scotch is also the best money can buy. Do you know why I have these? Lord knows there are cheaper cigars that are almost as good."

"I'm going to guess that you don't do second best."

"Very good. That's the way I run my business, and the way I live my life. I don't think I could find a better woman than my Madeline. Nope, nothing but the best for me. Set the bar high and don't accept disappointment."

I couldn't agree more. I had tried that motto, but life had kept me from achieving my dreams. Not to say I wasn't content with what I was doing, but I had always wanted more. Thing is, it was harder than one might think. Reaching for the stars meant sacrifice. I had lost too much as a teenager to give up any more.

Lawrence continued. "You listen like you'd like to join me."

"I've never been apposed to success." I took a puff.

"That's what I thought. I'm only asking because I've recently had an opportunity land in my lap. I feared I'd have to walk away from it and the thought sickened me. It's a sure thing."

"Is there such a thing as a sure thing?"

"Real-estate." He took a drink. "I've never lost on that one."

"How much do you need?"

"Let's not talk money. I'd rather talk investment. This is an office complex. It's been renovated and I'm hearing through the grapevine that the owner wants to unload it."

"Why?"

"He has several buildings. His problem is that he stretched himself a little too thin. He needs to cut his losses for the greater good. He makes nothing on this one, but gets to keep the others."

"Is that fair?"

"I know it doesn't feel like it, but we'd be helping him. He has to do this, and if it isn't us, it's somebody else."

"It's just that..."

"If you were to make the same mistake, he wouldn't hesitate to pounce on you. There is nothing personal here. It's business. If you prefer, we can put in a generous offer, depending on how much you have. I didn't act on this investment myself because I didn't want to make the same mistake and put myself in his shoes. I'm a lot more careful than that."

The point he made was a valid one. I'd always had the moral compass guiding me. Thing is, it hadn't taken care of me. We would be helping this guy, and although it didn't seem fair, it wasn't that terrible. All my life I'd made decisions that had held me back. I'd politely stepped out of the way so that others could reap the rewards. If I wanted to amount to something, I'd have to step it up.

"If you want something, Jon, you have to take it, especially if they came to you with a big shiny bow like this one did."

"You're right, and I'm interested."

"That's what I want to hear. I have a few photos of the place in a folder." He opened the drawer and shuffled through a few papers. He found two eight by ten photos. They were slid across to me.

I looked at them and saw a four-story building. "How many offices?"

"Thirty-two in total. With a ninety percent occupancy we should be able to pay the building off in about eight years. Then it's all passive income. Since the renovations have already been done, the overhead should be minimal. Like I said, it's a tough one to pass on."

"Then maybe we shouldn't."

"You are a smart man, Jon. No doubt you got that from our parents. I'll get to work on a contract tomorrow morning. Maybe you can come to my office and talk numbers. My office is in this building so I know first hand, this is a great deal. I'll give you a tour."

"That would be great." I got up and extended a hand. Lawrence quickly took it and gave it a firm shake. Then he tapped his glass against mine.

"To brothers," he toasted. "So that you don't have any doubts, I'll dig my birth certificate out. I'll get you a copy, for peace of mind."

"Thanks, Lawrence." I raised my glass. "To brothers."

Madeline and Ingrid were standing at the doorway of the study. I didn't notice them until Lawrence did. I smiled to Madeline, but her look was fearful.

Ingrid's was confusion. "You have a birth certificate?"

"This is family business you two. Could you give us a minute?" His smirk dared either of them to intercede. Ingrid saw it and although I'm sure she wanted to go toe to toe with him, she respected the fact that Madeline had to live with the man.

"I suppose we could get Nicolas ready for bed."

"That's a great idea," I added as I took a wine-dipped puff. "Send him in so that we can say good night."

They did, and my nephew gave me a pretty hearty hug. He asked if I would read him a story and I told him next time, that his mommy had her heart set on reading him one. He was okay with that as long as somebody was going to read one.

Coming tonight had magically filled a void, created by the loss of Rebecca and my parents. While I basked in the evening, Madeline looked worried. I was missing something. Lawrence had done well, and we were family. There was nothing for her to worry about.

The night rolled past nine by the time Nicolas fell asleep. We exchanged our good-bye hugs and made our way to the door. Promises had been made and I not only had a brother, I had a brother who was about to invest in our future. This man was going to turn our parent's money into a family business. It was an exciting turn of events.

Ingrid didn't even get the car door closed when the attack began. "What the hell happened back in there?"

Chapter twenty eight

I pulled out of my brother's driveway and let Ingrid stew on her question for a minute while I cut through the thicker traffic. Her stewing would hopefully bring her around. She had a temper, something that Marcus loved about her, but it wasn't a great tool for arguments. A couple blocks into the drive and I took my foot off the gas.

"I could ask you the same Ingrid. Why would you question him on having a birth certificate when he just offered to get me a copy, unless you were trying to piss him off?"

"Doesn't it all seem strange?"

"Of course it does. I never thought the night would end with me finding my brother. I mean, what are the odds?"

"About a billion to one so stop, take a deep breath, and think this through."

"If he produces a birth certificate then there's nothing to think through."

Ingrid crossed her arms and stared out the side window. I was right and she knew it. Fate didn't have to explain itself to us. We just needed to accept it. If he couldn't produce the paperwork to prove who he was, then that was a different story. He said he could.

Ingrid readied herself for the second round. "Do you remember why we went there?"

"Supper?"

"No. We wanted to see if the man who was married to Madeline was the kind of man who could put bruises on her wrist."

"Oh ya."

"What kind of man did you meet, Jon?"

"That's not fair. He's my brother. I don't want to judge him."

"Because maybe there's a bit of truth to the fact that he's no angel."

"I know he's no angel, but he loves her." He only wanted the best and Madeline was that. I had the other half of those twins and could vouch for Rebecca.

"Did you see the way she cowered around him? She ran around getting his drink, cooking his food, being careful not to say anything that might upset him. She almost crawled out of her skin when I asked about the birth certificate. I'll bet he's giving her shit for inviting me as we speak."

I thought about that and had to disagree. He loved her and wanted her to be on the same page. He didn't choose her because she was feisty like Ingrid. He chose her because she understood who he was and why they had the success they did. Maybe they'd be talking, he'd be getting her back on that page.

"You shouldn't assume, Ingrid."

"And you shouldn't be so damn trusting. Promise me you won't do anything stupid. You have a good chunk of money and it doesn't hurt to hold onto it until you know what you want to do with it."

"I agree."

When I pulled into the parking lot she invited me up, so I parked the car. Marcus would be there and he had brought a home-made German Kuchen. His aunt had been in Paris and had dropped it off. It was impossible to say no.

He started to cut the cake as soon as we walked into the room. "How was the visit?"

I blurted it out. "I have a brother."

Marcus looked over to Ingrid as if I was high or drunk. Maybe she could explain. She simply shrugged. "The husband used to be Georg Falkman until he was adopted. Says he has a birth certificate to prove it."

"No shit." Marcus had the same reaction as I did. It was the reaction the girls should have had. "What are the chances?"

"Ingrid says a billion to one."

He nodded. "Probably even high, but who cares. You found him. That's awesome news."

Ingrid remained on the fence. "The man wants to invest Jon's money."

I corrected her. "My money and his. He has a right to half of it."

Marcus quickly jumped on the Ingrid bandwagon. "Whoa, Buddy. That's your money. That guy wasn't around all those years. He never even met them. He was given up at birth."

"That's the thing. He wasn't a runaway. They gave him up."

Marcus grappled to understand. "Doesn't this guy have his own money?"

"Lots of it," I answered. "That's why I trust him."

"If he's got his own then he can use his and you can use some of yours and bank the rest. Hell, invest it in my business. We can be partners."

"I appreciate your concern, but this guy does this for a living." I turned to Ingrid. "Did they not have a magnificent house?"

"It was okay," she admitted.

"Any house in Paris is magnificent." I corrected. "Their house is all that and then some. They even have a driveway."

That shut them up, and so it should have. Lawrence had done very well for himself, a man given up at birth. I was impressed even if they were not.

I enjoyed the silence as we all ate our dessert. I took their silence as a sign that I was right to be investing with this guy. Not only was this my brother, and good at what he was doing, but he'd stopped the voices from the critics.

"This Kuchen is delicious." I stuffed the last bite in my mouth as I remembered Heidi. "I gotta run."

Marcus was ready to cut me another slice. "What's up?"

"Nothing, just an early day tomorrow. I want to get my apartment fixed up. I was stupid to tear it apart. I just made a bunch of work for myself."

"Stay for a beer."

I started for the door and continued my lie. "Wish I could. The place isn't going to fix itself."

Ingrid muttered something about running any money matters past her before I commit, but the door closed before she could finish. I loved the fact that she cared, didn't love the fact that she thought this was her place.

I kept an eye on the time while I dodged and dove through the traffic. I was running late. Good thing she'd have to get off the plane, grab her luggage and find her way through customs.

The traffic thickened, slowing me down. "Damn." If I was late, she'd be pissed.

I finally hit the off ramp and rolled into the airport. I passed a cube van and drove far too fast down the Arrivals lane. Then I saw her. She was sitting on a small suitcase as if she'd been waiting a while.

Chapter twenty nine

Heidi sat on her suitcase looking like one of Marcus's models. She had the large sunglasses and the big floppy purple hat. She looked calm amongst all the madness of an airport. Taxi cabs were racing around, honking and flashing headlights. Cars, like mine, were double-parked and people shuffled around her as if she was a homeless person begging for spare change.

"I'm sorry I'm late." She didn't know how sorry I was. The last thing I needed was another argument. And then there was the cab that pulled up behind me. He gave a quick honk.

She got up and let me give her a hug. "No big. Good to see you, Jon."

"Were you waiting long?"

"Five minutes. Traffic heavy?" She reached down for the handle of her suitcase.

I beat her to it and picked it up. "In spots. I'm really sorry for being late."

The cab driver honked again, this time a single steady blast.

She looked over to him and then away. "Don't worry about it."

I opened her door and let her get in before throwing the suitcase in the back seat. Then I ran around to the driver's side, got in and sped off. That made the cab driver happy.

"Good flight?"

"They had beer, if that's what you mean."

"Is that why you're not mad at me?"

"I'm not angry, Jon, although it would have been nice if you would have brought the kids."

I laughed. If she was joking around, she was okay. "Have you eaten?"

"Not in a couple days."

That threw me. It wasn't like she was a big eater, but it wasn't like her to go that long. "I'm renovating my apartment so I'm staying at a hotel. They have a great restaurant."

"Could we order room service? I don't feel like hanging out with people."

"I suppose. Is everything okay?"

"Not really, but I can explain over supper. Now that I'm here, I have my appetite back. I'm actually starving."

"Schnitzel Starving?"

"Prime rib, potatoes and gravy starving. We should order extra buns, extra gravy."

"Are you pregnant?" I regretted asking that the moment it came out. Not that it would have anything to do with me, but I'd seldom seen her eat like that.

"Very funny. Babies require sex. I've been keeping myself off the market. I don't want to be dating the idiots I work with, and I'd hate to drag a regular guy into this mess."

"I didn't mean anything by asking that. It's just the heavy eating."

"I know. Hey, is it okay for me to stay with you. If not, I can get my own place. I just can't do it in my name. I'm flying under the radar for a couple days, and I hope you didn't tell anybody I was coming."

"I didn't." Who would I tell? Marcus, Ingrid and Eddy would have freaked out if they knew. I was glad to hear she wanted the secrecy and didn't want to visit with them.

"How's your dad doing?"

She did a very slow and deliberate head turn. If I could have seen her eyes through the dark glass they would have been giving me stink eye.

"Never mind."

I pulled into the parking lot and we quietly made our way to my room. She threw her suitcase on the bed that hadn't been slept in yet. I picked up the phone and ordered our food. It was late, but the kitchen was open twenty-four hours.

Heidi opened her suitcase and pulled out a more comfortable outfit. "I'll be a couple minutes. I just need a hot bath. Is that okay?"

"Sure. The food will be twenty minutes. Take your time."

While she soaked, I tried to clean up the room. I didn't have a lot here, but it seemed to be spread around pretty good. I pulled the covers up on my bed, stacked the pillows and started to look through the channels on the television. I'd finally found something to watch when there was a knock on the door. The food was here.

Everything got set out on her bed. There was no counter space and eating off the floor wasn't an option. We'd eat on my bed.

"Food's here." I wasn't sure what to call this. It wasn't supper anymore than it was breakfast at this hour, and it was a little much for a midnight snack.

"Be right out."

I waited a minute and she appeared looking a lot happier. Her hair was wet and looked a lot more burgundy that auburn. She had found one of the hotel housecoats and wrapped herself up in white plush.

"Better not get gravy on that."

She started to untie the belt. "I can take it off."

I blushed and she stopped. "That's what I thought. Did you get extra buns?"

"I did."

She dug into one and that was when I noticed the black eye had really darkened. It seemed to be spreading to the other eye. I didn't say anything. Instead I watched her as she dumped extra gravy on the potatoes. Her eyes closed at the first bite and she didn't open them or take a breath until she was done chewing.

I wasn't hungry so I sat back and tried to guess where she was putting it all. She had a way. Once, when she was twelve, I bet her she couldn't eat ten pancakes. She ate sixteen. She had lunch two hours later, yet she'd always been a petite girl. Again I looked

Johannes

at those eyes, so gentle and yet so fierce. There was no way that shiner should have been drifting into the second eye.

"What happened?"

She stopped for a second to bat her eyes at me. "It's getting good, right?"

"He hit you again, didn't he?"

"No." She hesitated, not wanting to lie to me. "He has people to do this for him, remember?"

"What did you do?"

"Like I have to do anything." Again, she remembered it was me she was talking to. "I pissed him off and he had Danny beat me up."

"Danny? I can't believe he'd ever hurt you."

"He didn't have a choice. Dad knew Danny always thought of me like a little sister. The man would protect me with his life. That was why he had to do it."

"Did he break your nose? I'm just asking because the other eye is darkening."

"I did that with a book. Danny could never hit me in the face."

"So he did other stuff?"

Heidi put her plate down on nightstand and stood up. "Now don't be mad when I show you. This was a test and Danny had to pass or Dad would have gone after his family. I don't blame him and actually had to beg him to do a good job. I love his wife. She's such a sweetheart and as innocent as them come. She didn't need this."

She untied the robe, but held it closed. "Promise me you won't freak out."

"How do I...?"

"Promise me!"

"Okay. I promise."

"And I'm going to hold you to it." Heidi pulled the left side of her robe open revealing her left leg, hip and upper body. I expected my eyes to go straight to her exposed breast, but they didn't. I was mesmerised at the bruising on her ribs, her shoulder and knee. I tried not to look too surprised. She gave me a second, closed the robe and opened the right side. The ribs weren't as

111

bruised, but her leg was purple and black from the hip down to her ankle.

I was speechless as I got up, set my plate down on the other bed and walked toward her. She'd been trying to fight back the tears. She finally gave in to them. Her robe fell open when she held her arms open for the hug she'd likely wanted since the airport. I slipped my hands inside that robe and pulled her in close.

"I'm gonna kill your father." This time I meant it.

"Shh. I don't want to hear you talking like that. You're my prince and I want you to ride a white horse."

"Ya but…"

"But nothing. I'm safe here and I need my prince to hold me, not be some dumb hero. Hero's are idiots."

I held her and kissed her forehead as she cried. I'd never seen her cry before. I'd seen her beat up, I'd seen her hurt so bad that she had to miss school, but I'd never seen her broken.

Chapter thirty

Heidi and I never talked after the hug. Instead I let her crawl into my bed and curl up against me. She let me hold her for an hour before finally falling asleep. I was still holding her when we woke up the next morning.

She looked up to me with her racoon eyes. "Morning."

I placed a gentle kiss on the end of her nose. "You became naked at some point."

"This is becoming a bit of a habit with me. Sorry about that."

"We used to look forward to moments like this."

"You were a horny teenager back then." She winked. "Right?"

"Definitely."

"Did you order coffee yet?"

I gave my arm a wiggle. It was trapped under her. "Kinda hard to get up."

She cringed in pain as she lifted herself off my arm. I pulled it free and slipped out of bed. My pants were being pulled over my underwear when she whistled. "And I thought the buns last night were good."

I turned around to see her trying to sit up. The covers had dropped to her waist and this time my eyes gravitated to her chest. It was hard not to stare. She noticed and covered up. "I thought you weren't interested."

"I uh, was, uh, looking at your ribs."

"Sure you were. I remember that look. We were kids and spent a lot of time hiding from reality in the sheets of your bed. It worked if I remember right. You always took me to a magical place. Was it magical for you?"

"Don't be silly." My face flushed. "You know it was. Hey, did you break any ribs?"

"No, but I paid the doctor to say I did in his report. That way if Dad saw them it would put a smile on his face."

"That's messed up."

"That's my Dad." She shifted her butt around to get comfortable. "Coffee?"

"I was getting there, but then I got distracted."

She smiled. "Glad I've still got it. They say it gets harder the older you get."

"You're thirty two." I dialled room service. "You're not old."

"Not a teenager either. Can I get french toast?"

"Not pancakes?"

"Really, Jon. I'm in France." It seemed like a no-brainer. "Do you have any plans today?"

"I have to swing by an office this morning? Is that okay?"

"Of course."

Looked over, I caught Heidi out of the corner of my eye. She was holding the sheets back and checking the bruising.

"I have to leave in an hour. What are you looking at?"

"Danny did an amazing job. He messed me up good and yet I don't feel all that sore. He really is a loyal soldier."

"How can you say that? The man beat you up."

"No. He just became my number one."

"You sound like you're in charge."

"Someday. My Dad made a lot of enemies when he had me beat up. That being said, they're more scared of him now than they've ever been."

"Doesn't that put Danny in danger?"

"I made a few calls. Nobody touches him."

"I'm sure glad you're here and not there."

"Because I'm in your bed and I'm naked?"

I shook my head as I slipped on a clean shirt. She was in good spirits after all that she'd been through. I wanted to ask how long she needed to hide out but decided against it. She was a good friend and I loved the playfulness. Heidi always made me feel special and who didn't like that? I ducked in the bathroom, shaved, and got out just in time to answer the door.

"Your french toast, ma lady." I brought them over to her before she decided to expose that naked body again. "Don't get up."

"Thank you, my prince. Will you be gone long?" Again she shifted around and the covers dropped. I tried not to look and she rolled her eyes at my modesty.

"This is a business meeting. I should be back by noon."

"Don't race back for me. If it's okay, I'm just going to sit around and watch television. I don't plan on leaving the room. So what business are you doing?"

"Oh that's right. You don't know. I found my brother. He's Madeline's husband. Can you imagine the coincidence?"

"Madeline is…"

"Rebecca's sister."

She dipped her eyebrows and it killed any playfulness. "You mean this guy has been in your life all this time and you never knew it until now?"

"Crazy, huh?"

"I wouldn't use that word. Have you seen a birth certificate?"

"He said he'd dig it out for me today. Were buying a building together. I'm getting a tour."

"I think you need to slam on the brakes, my prince. This all sounds a little…"

"Not you too."

"So I'm not the only one that thinks this is far too convenient?"

"Marcus, Ingrid and Madeline are sceptics."

"So why aren't you listening to them?" She gave me a split second to talk and then cut me off. "Because you are the great Johannes Weisman. You get your mind set on something and there's no stopping you. I tried to stop you from becoming one of my father's mules and what did you say?"

"Easy money."

"Easy money, except it wasn't that easy, was it?" Again she cut me off. "Just get the information and let me go over it. I'm a whiz with business and I can spot a problem a mile away. And what's this guy's name? I'll make a couple calls, discretely of course."

"Lawrence Trembley, and we'll talk about it when I get back. Is that okay?"

"Just looking out for you."

Naked, badly bruised and eating pancakes in my bed. I wanted to ask her how she was looking out for me. If any of my friends found out she was here I'd never hear the end of it. If Rebecca's sister or her parents ever found out about her, they'd never forgive me. That being said, because of her I hadn't had a lot of time to feel sorry for myself.

"Just do me one favour. Let me know what he wants," she asked.

"That's easy," I answered. "He wants a brother."

"That's not how it works, Jon. He's a businessman first. Always remember that."

Chapter thirty one

The first thing I noticed about the office building was the new siding and how clean it looked. Lawrence met me downstairs in the lobby and brought me up to his office. It was a corner one on the fourth floor. He had a nice view.

"Can I apologise for Ingrid's birth certificate comment? She worries about me."

"No you cannot. There is no crime in having friends that care. Let's face it, this is a little bit of a weird situation. We just met and yet we want to start up a Property Management Company." He slid an envelope over to me.

I opened it to see a birth certificate. It read Georg Manuel Falkman. I studied it for a couple of minutes before giving Lawrence a hug. "So do I call you Georg or Lawrence?"

"I probably wouldn't know who you were talking to if you said Georg. I've been a Lawrence most of my life. You can keep that one. It's a legal copy."

He took a spot behind his desk and went straight to business. He had legal documents for our offer already drafted up. The price, I was told, was a good one, but still steep. On the way over I'd received a call and there'd been an offer put on the house and I'd accepted it. With that money added, I could cover the costs of this venture. I signed the papers and gave my real-estate agent's information to Lawrence. He said he had people that could fast-track the sale. We needed that money sooner than later.

He also had a contract sitting there for the start of our Company. We'd be the Trembley-Weisman Brothers. It had a nice ring to it. He originally thought Weisman Brothers, but being given away, he was never a Weisman.

I understood and signed the documents.

"Eight years," Lawrence chuffed. "You'll be able to retire."

He slid a piece of paper in front of me. It was half of what the rent paid. At first I thought it was the whole amount, but he quickly corrected me.

I thought about Heidi and knew she'd be angry that I didn't consult her, but she wasn't my wife. I'm pretty sure I was doing the right thing. It was all of my parent's money, but they didn't need it. They were gone. I didn't need to worry about Rebecca's opinion anymore. I'd visited her at the cemetery. No, this was my money and I could do with it whatever I wanted. I wanted to start a Property Management Company called Trembley-Weisman. It felt right.

Lawrence saw me drift away to the what-ifs of my future and started to round up the papers and sign them himself.

I continued to think about what I'd just done. It wasn't like I needed anything or a place to stay. I had my apartment and since I was doing the renovations, it wouldn't cost more than a few supplies. To invest everything was maybe better. I'd just spend it, maybe squander some of it. Ingrid and Marcus said it themselves. I wasn't good with money.

Lawrence and I spent the next two hours going over a few more details. We talked about where we wanted to be in the future. We covered the rent hikes, our long-term tenants, and whether I wanted an office. It would be free of charge, of course. I had to call Heidi to let her know I was running late.

Around three o'clock a young woman walked in. She had alabaster skin and long lovely red hair.

"Is it that time already?" Lawrence asked her.

"It is."

"One second, Scarlett. I'm just wrapping things up here."

She politely left and I found myself watching her leave.

Lawrence laughed. "She's a cute thing, isn't she? I'm thinking of bringing her on as an intern. What do you think?"

"I think you could do worse. How do you concentrate around someone like that?"

He got up from his chair. "I'm a professional."

I walked out and Scarlett joined us for the elevator ride down to the lobby. Outside I went my way and they went theirs. I imagine he was taking her on a late luncheon to go over her credentials. If she was half as good as she looked she would get the job.

On the way back to the hotel I picked up a little gift for Heidi. I wasn't sure why I was buying her anything other than I appreciated the fact that she was filling a void. I'd lost Rebecca and if it weren't for Heidi I'd be a mess. I'd feel like shit and likely sit around feeling sorry for myself. Heidi wouldn't allow that.

When I walked in the door, Heidi had planned a surprise of her own.

The room was lit up entirely with candles. "What's this?"

"Good you're home." She'd had a card table set up in the corner. There was a candle in the centre. There was also a white table cloth and fine china. There were water glasses, wine glasses and cloth napkins. "Sit."

I did as I was told.

Then she opened a bag that had been wrapped in a bath towel. She reached in and pulled out something that I hadn't seen since I left Stuttgart. I'm not sure if I ever knew the proper name of these things, but I called them jiggers. It was a square of bread dough, filled with hamburger, sauerkraut, onion and bacon, closed up and baked in the oven. My grandmother used to make them all the time, when she was still alive.

She dropped it on my plate, followed by a second and third. She took two for herself. "Dig in."

"Where did you find these?" I picked it up with my hand and took a bite. "Oh ya. That's exactly it."

"They're good?"

I gave her a thumbs up as I stuffed another bite into my mouth.

She started in on hers, but stopped to pour the wine. It was a hefty pour. I didn't care and took a good swig. I finished the glass as the second jigger disappeared. She topped my glass up and I started in on the third jigger. There were twelve of them in the bag and I'd have six of them. I'd also downed three generous glasses of wine and starting on my forth. Good thing she bought two bottles.

"Oh, you are an angel. I don't know how you did it, but that was amazing. What a great day. First I start a Company with my brother, and now I have the best meal I've ever had."

"Best?" A grin spread across her face. "Was it because of the food or the company?"

"Both." I slurred as I finished my fourth glass. In my defence I hadn't eaten anything all day. "Now I have a gift for you."

I pulled out the bag of marshmallows. They were coconut-coated, pink and the first thing I'd ever bought her. She was eight and we ate the whole bag in one sitting. It cemented a lifelong friendship.

She took one and bit into it. I swear her eyes sparkled while she chewed. "You remembered."

"We've been best friends ever since." It was a nostalgic gift, much like her jiggers were. Maybe it was the wine, but suddenly the last decade of our lives disappeared. I was twenty again and we were as solid as the day we ate those first marshmallows...maybe better.

She got up to give me a hug. I got up and let her. She felt good in my arms...too good.

She looked up into my eyes and seeing that I'd drank just the right amount of wine, decided to kiss me. I kissed her back. The kiss lasted several minutes, like a proper kiss should. Her lips were silky soft and as eager as when we were teenagers.

She broke the embrace, pushed me back and started to unbutton her blouse. It dropped to the floor, followed by her bra. She walked backward, toward the bathroom, while she unbuttoned her pants. They were slipped off at the door. She was naked.

"I have a bath poured. Do you care to join me?"

I had fought the guilt, fought the emotions, and fought our memories long enough. I'd been sober and grieving. I had wanted to feel bad, wanted to suffer, but I didn't want to suffer anymore.

My shirt landed on the bed and my pants in a tangle on the floor with hers. I got into the tub first and she slipped in with her back against my chest. My arms slipped around her bruised body and she melted against me.

For a few minutes we just sat there taking in the moment. We deserved this. Then she put her right hand on my hip, partially spun around and kissed me. I enjoyed her kiss enough to move my hand over her left breast. I cupped it as if it were as fragile as a snowflake.

Her hand slipped from my hip to the part of me that had been growing against her backside. That ended the kiss and sobered me like a slap across the face.

"I can't," I gasped as I pushed her forward and pulled her hand away. "What are we doing?"

"I thought I was getting you drunk so that we could have tub sex."

"I'm sorry, Heidi." I got myself free and grabbed a towel. She fell on her side, slopping water and suds on the floor. "This isn't right. You deserve better."

She got out of the tub, towelled off and wrapped herself in a robe. I was already under the covers. "I'm the one who's sorry, Jon. I forget that you're different than most men. While that's what I like about you, it's also what I hate about you. It's the one thing I'd never try to change about you. And for the record, I'd be proud to have you."

"You don't think I'm strange?"

"For not wanting to get it on with a racoon? Yes, you're strange, but it's what makes you, you." She scrunched her face. "Are we good?"

"Always."

She bit down on her lip. "Can I still sleep in your bed?"

"Only if you get dressed and promise me you'll stay that way."

She got up, grabbed some sweat pants and a t-shirt out of her suitcase and headed for the bathroom. "You're a tough nut to crack, Jon Weisman." She stopped at the door, put a hand on the jamb and leaned back. "But there's always tomorrow."

"Really?"

"Sorta kidding."

"I don't know how much more I can take."

"Good to know. I'm beginning to go a little cross-eyed, if you know what I mean."

Chapter thirty two

Lawrence called me first thing in the morning. He wanted to tell me that the sale of the house had been finalised. There was nothing further to sign and he had arranged for a moving company to pick up the last of the personal belongings and put them in storage. There were a few things to sign as far as the Company went, but they wouldn't be ready today.

That was exciting news and it helped me push Heidi out of my head, not that I pushed her far. She was beautiful, even with the black eyes and the purple ribs, and she was sweet on me. Given a chance to grieve, I'd probably jump at the chance to have her back in my life. For now, I just wanted to remember Rebecca.

I left Heidi back at the hotel. She was sleeping and looking better than she should. I needed fresh air and fresh thoughts. Eddy's theatre was a couple blocks away and what better way to free my mind but in the fantasy of the movie world.

My favourite coffee shop was on the corner so I stopped for a specialty one. I ordered a vanilla latte. Not sure whether I like the coffee more or the paper cups. They were black and purple and didn't burn the fingers.

The movie theatre was just up the street when I ran into Eddy. He was on his way to my hotel and he was frantic. "Jon. I'm so glad I found you."

"I was looking for you too. What's up?"

"He's here."

That wasn't a lot to go on and I couldn't tell if his excitement was good or bad. "Who's here?"

"Joseph. I saw him."

"What. Here in Paris?"

"About ten minutes ago. I'm sure it was him."

I had no doubt it was. "Shit. Heidi's here. He's after her."

"What's Heidi doing here?"

I didn't answer. Instead I started back for the hotel. It was a fast walk at first, but soon broke into a run. Eddy chased after me, asking the same question.

The door was ajar when we got there and the room was empty. It was easy to tell by the knocked over chair and broken lamp, that there'd been a struggle.

"Answer me Jon," Eddy demanded.

"She got beat up. Told me her father was out and taking the business back."

"Taking it back? What the hell was she doing with it?"

I shrugged. "They've got her."

"And now they want us. Damn it, Jon. How long has she been here?"

"Couple days."

"And you didn't think to tell anyone? What did she want?"

"She didn't want anything."

"Bullshit. That girl always has an angle." He walked over and grabbed her shirt off the bed. "She's playing you, my friend."

I suddenly wondered about that. I was so busy being flattered by her playful charm that I wasn't looking at anything objectively. But this was Heidi, and she was her father's daughter. Like it or not, she was born looking for an angle.

The phone rang and I answered it.

"Hi Jon, it's me." She sounded scared.

"Where are you?"

"I'm at the Luxembourg Gardens. You have to come get me."

I wasn't sure if it needed saying, but I did anyway. "Your Dad's in town."

"You're cute. Just come get me."

I hung up. "Okay. We're off to the Luxembourg Gardens." I don't know why I thought he'd just follow and want to help, but I did. I expected him to be as concerned as I was. Growing up, all we had was each other. Granted, lots had changed, but it was still Heidi. That was the problem. I had seen her differently than the others.

"You're on your own, Buddy."

"What?"

"She's up to something. She's always up to something."

"You should have seen her. She was black and blue, and I don't mean just a wrist or an eye. It was her ribs, hips…"

"And how'd you see all that?" He put his hands up as if making his point.

"It was nothing like that," although it was exactly like that. "I'm going."

"Ah crap." He followed me out the door.

I had a feeling he'd come around. We were tight as kids. There was nothing we wouldn't do for each other, or Heidi. Being the only girl she had it a little harder. We incorrectly deemed her the weakest of the group because she was small and often did things that made us look bad. The truth was that she was a powerhouse. Always the adorable and seemingly innocent one, she was never afraid to get her hands dirty for us.

"What if it's a trap?" Eddy asked.

I hadn't thought about that. I was definitely thinking about that when we got off the Metro. It had to be the two men that were waiting for us.

They flashed their guns and book-ended us as we walked south, down the sidewalk. They stopped in front of a small restaurant and shoved us through the front door. Heidi was sitting at one of the back tables. She wasn't alone.

"I'm sorry guys. I didn't mean to get you involved."

"Right." Eddy took a seat across from her. "What game are you playing?"

"Shut up," the thug beside her demanded. He wasn't in the mood for any crap. "Where's Marcus?"

Eddy answered. "How the hell would we know?"

"Joseph wants to see all of you."

Again, Eddy held his own. "Well we don't want to see him. What are you going to do, shoot us?"

"Those were my orders," the man replied. "I guess we need insurance. We'll keep the girl a little longer."

"Shit. You can have her." Eddy had heard enough and tried to get up. He was stuffed back into the chair.

"Okay smart ass. Here's how it's going to work. Joseph is angry with you four, but he's willing to forgive and forget. This is a golden opportunity for you. You do him a small favour and he'll forget you lot ever existed."

"We're not moving anymore drugs for him."

"I said small, not minuscule. Be at the Arc de Triomphe in an hour and he'll tell you what he wants. You'd be smart to show, and bring Marcus. He's a part of this too. If not, you'll be reading about this little beauty in tomorrow's newspaper."

We all waited for Eddy's response, but it never came.

"Get out of here."

The men behind us lifted us out of our chairs and escorted us out.

Eddy and I started for the Metro. "What do you figure, Eddy?"

"Oh, we're going, you and me. Marcus doesn't need to know about this just yet."

"What do you think he wants?"

"A war."

Chapter thirty three

We stopped by the theatre, even though it wasn't on the way. Eddy wanted to pick up a pair of binoculars. I wanted to ask why, but found myself in a bit of a cloud. This wasn't really happening, was it?

There was a Metro a block away from the attraction where Joseph wanted us to meet him and we were fifteen minutes early. Eddy hurried me along the Champs-Élysées and in to a hotel. "I know the owner, did some work for him. I need to get on the roof and I'm sure he'll let us."

He rang the bell at the front desk and a man appeared from the back. "Do you need a room?"

"I need your boss, Pierre. Is he around?" Eddy asked.

"He's in a meeting. Can I help you?"

Eddy only took a second to come up with a story. "I was here a week or two back doing some work. I think I may have left a few things up on the roof. Do you mind if I check it out?"

"I can't leave the..."

"That's okay. I'll take the contractor's key and return it in ten. I just need my snap drill."

"I uh." The request seemed to be innocent enough and he was afraid to ask what a snap drill was. He opened the drawer and retrieved a key. "Ten minutes?"

"Not even. Thanks."

Luckily, Eddy was still in his work clothes. He looked like he was about to knock out a window or grout a sink.

The man at the desk didn't ask, but I did. "Snap drill?"

"The element of confusion. Nobody wants to be that guy."

We took the elevator to the top floor and then the stairs to the rooftop. The view was spectacular and we had a clear sight line to the Arc de Triomphe. Eddy watched as Joseph stood there with Heidi and the three thugs. He lifted the binoculars up and had a better look. Heidi was being held tight by one of the men. Every time she struggled he would give her a shake to smarten her up. It wasn't working.

"Okay. We have the three from before and Joseph. The hired help has guns, but I don't think Joseph is packing. He'd be a fool to breach his probation. That just leaves Heidi. Do you know if she's got a gun?"

"I don't think so, but she's on our side."

"Don't assume anything, Jon. I still don't trust her. Doesn't matter. We can't take them so we need to get down there and hear what he has to say." He watched them for another five minutes. "We should go."

Inside the Arc you could take the stairs to the top. There were only two stairwells, which could trap us.

"You should let me do the talking," Eddy suggested.

"What do you think he wants us to do?"

"It'll be something crazy, something we won't be able to do. He wants us to rot in prison like he did."

We dropped the key off at the front desk and Eddy acted the part of the disappointed contractor. He had lost his snap drill, likely for good.

Outside we had to take the tunnel to the Arc. You'd never make your way through the traffic circle. It was twelve lanes of dense traffic, honking horns and desperation. Cars wove their way around it in a dance that rivalled the running of the bulls.

The tunnel came out under the Arc and we headed for the stairs on the right. They were artistic, square and somewhat cold. For some reason the tourists loved them. Looking down from above, I got it.

128

Stepping out into the open you could see all of Paris, from the creamy domes of the Sacré-Cœur to the Eiffel Tower. You could see the route Napoleon's troops took on their way back to the Palace (Louvre), through the Arc de Triomphe and down the Champs-Élysées. You could also see Joseph and Heidi, backstopped by the three stooges.

"So glad you showed up," Joseph said as he took a step toward us.

"Yes," Eddy answered. "It's been a while."

"Ten years, eleven months and fourteen days, but who's counting?"

"I'm just glad we're not bitter." Eddy pushed for a reaction. He wanted to see him lose his cool. Joseph prided himself on his control.

"You're a funny man, Mr Cruiser. Where's Marcus? I was looking forward to seeing him too."

I answered. We didn't need Eddy pushing him over the edge. "We haven't told him. He's working and we didn't have enough time to fill him in."

"I'm disappointed."

"Get used to it," Eddy chuffed. "Are you in on this, Heidi?"

She shook her head. Maybe I was blind, but I could tell she wasn't a part of this. She wasn't getting anything from Joseph.

"I have a proposition for you guys, a gesture that would allow me to have no hard feelings. You do this and I promise I'll forget you lot even exist."

"And if we don't?"

"Then you exist." Joseph turned and punched Heidi in the gut. "And I'd have hard feelings."

The thug to Heidi's right grabbed two handfuls of her shirt as she doubled over, lifted her off her feet and shoved her over the edge. He let go with one hand, causing her to latch on to him with both of hers.

He held her out at arm's length and looked over his shoulder to Joseph for further instructions.

Chapter thirty four

Heidi dangled over the edge like a tangled up wind chime. At a hundred and thirty pounds, the man managed to hold her without too much effort. His face didn't strain as he stared at Joseph for further instruction. If Joseph nodded one way the man would shake her free and let her drop to her death. A different gesture might bring her back to safety.

Joseph looked at me. "It's a hundred and sixty-two feet. What do you think her chances are?"

I nodded. "We'll do it."

Joseph motioned for the man to pull Heidi back onto the rooftop. He did, but didn't let go of her shirt. The need for tossing her over hadn't been extinguished yet. Joseph wanted to enlighten us with a story first.

"Prison wasn't so bad. It's a great place to find oneself," he started.

Eddy was getting ready to say something witty, so I elbowed him in the ribs. Joseph nodded a thank you of sorts and continued.

"Listening to other people's stories, what they did and how they got caught, it really helped me to understand that I'd kept myself small and safe. I had money, but the cash isn't success. To be a true success you must always be growing. Growth is power and power is security. The bigger you are, the less chance anybody will be foolish enough to double cross you or steal your territory.

Good thing for you I'm a work in progress. While I should kill you four and hang your bodies in the tree in front of my house, I'm going to offer you a chance to make amends."

"Is he for real?" Eddy asked.

Again I elbowed him and let Joseph continue. Eddy was always lousy at math. We were outnumbered and they had guns, not to mention arms big enough to crush us.

"You surprise me, Jon," Joseph admitted. "I feel you should be the one in charge of this mission. My daughter cannot be trusted, your friend here is too emotional, and Marcus, he didn't even show up."

"We haven't told him yet."

"Well you best get on that. It'll take the four of you to pull this off."

I had to ask. "What is this?"

"We had books in prison, all kinds of books. I liked to study the arts. I'd spend my days studying paintings, statues and other cultures. I found it fascinating."

Eddy didn't want to hear anymore. "What do you want?"

"Get to the point," Joseph laughed. "I can do that. I want a Van Gogh."

That caught me off guard. "Like a Vincent Van Gogh, the painter."

"I'm so glad you understand. You really should be the one leading your merry band of thieves.'

"But we're not thieves," I told him.

"And yet you idiots took all those years from me. You see how I might have made the mistake of thinking you could pull this off."

"How are we going to steal a painting?"

"Not just any painting. I want the Café Terrace at Night. It's at the Louvre."

"The Louvre? That place is a fortress."

"That's not my problem."

"We'll get caught," I told him. "We're not art thieves."

"Here's the thing." He motioned for the man to drag Heidi back over the ledge so that she could join the others. "If, by the grace of God, you manage to steal this piece, I'll have a painting worth a few million dollars. It'll cover the wages I would have made while I was in prison. If you fail, you'll all rot in jail, like I did. That might be a more fitting outcome, don't you think?"

Eddy dodged my elbow. "So this isn't about us stealing a painting. It's about us going to jail."

"It's about me being in a 'win win' situation."

"And us in a 'lose lose'."

"Not at all. Steal the painting and you'll have paid your debt. Go to jail and you've paid your debt. Refuse this, or run and I'll hunt you down. You won't be able to hide."

I could imagine the bars on the windows, the orange overalls for formal wear. We couldn't accomplish this, yet we'd have to try. What choice did we have? "How many days do we have?"

"You'll have a couple days. I plan on leaving as soon as I can."

"Seriously?" Eddy took a step toward Joseph and was cut off by two of the thugs. "You're a madman."

"A little angry, yes. If you don't understand now, I'm sure you will in about ten years."

"This isn't fair," I added. "Why don't you just kick the shit out of us, like you did to your daughter?"

Heidi put her hands into my chest and shoved me toward the stairs. "Let's get out of here, Jon."

"No." I stood up to her. "I asked a valid question. Why'd you do this to her?"

"I didn't."

"No, your henchmen did."

Joseph laughed. "Are you worried about my daughter's well-being?"

"Let's go, Jon." She continued to back me out of earshot. "Enough."

"What the…"

Heidi shook her head. "I don't need him knowing you still care about me. Makes me a target. It's better if he thinks you hate me."

"Why?"

"He'll beat me beyond anything he's done in the past. I'll become leverage to get you to do whatever he wants."

"That's crazy."

"Shove me to the ground, like you don't want me touching you."

"No, I..."

"Do it." She shoved me again and I stumbled.

"Get away from me." I shoved her back and she fell hard. I cringed knowing she landed on her bruised hip. It didn't help to see Eddy step over her on his way to the exit. His knee almost caught her cheek.

She winced as she got to one knee. "Fuck you both."

I wanted to help her up. Instead, I walked away. She caught up with us on the stairs. "Good job. Thanks."

Chapter thirty five

The Metro took us back to my apartment. On the train Eddy wouldn't sit with us. I tried to talk to him, get him to come around, but he wasn't ready. He needed to get over his anger and ease his way into this. He also had to rationalise Heidi hanging around with me, Joseph thinking he could get away with this, and how we'd get Marcus to play along?

"Let him stew, Jon. We need to come up with a plan."

"We need to talk to Marcus. Whether he knows it or not, he's involved."

"Where is he?"

"He's at a photo-shoot in Montmartre. He wanted to use the flowery setting of Musée de la Vie Romantique for a local author's book launch advertisement."

"And you know where this place is?"

"I told him about it."

"Are we on the right train?" she asked.

"No. We have to get off at the next stop. Then we go north."

"Hear that Eddy?" Heidi yelled over to him. "We're going to visit Marcus. Wanna come?"

He was either hard of hearing or ignoring us. She dropped her head on my shoulder. "We'll go without him."

I let her rest her head on me. When we got up to leave, Eddy came with us. He didn't say anything, still trying to figure a way out of this mess.

Me, I was still trying to figure out what this mess was. "Are we really thinking of doing this?"

Heidi didn't hesitate. "Of course we are."

Eddy broke his silence. "You're as crazy as your old man."

"No. I'm a woman that ran a big drug cartel. That means I have connections. I just have to see if any of them are going to be helpful."

"So we swap a pound of heroin for a painting?" Eddy chuffed. "Is that how it works?"

"No," she answered as we boarded the next train. "But I know people that could advise us. We need all the help we can get."

I asked again, "We're doing this?"

"Soon as possible." She stopped to get our attention. "I'm serious. My father will hunt us down. There's nowhere to hide. We have a much better chance trying to steal a painting."

"It's the damn Louvre," I reminded her. "We might as well steal the Mona Lisa and the Statue of David while we're there."

"Don't be silly, Jon. Statues are too heavy." Her smile lightened the mood and even turned the corner of Eddy's mouth upward.

The train travelled a few blocks and when it stopped, we got off. The station wasn't that far from Marcus's photo-shoot.

When he saw us he dropped his camera down to his hip. "What the hell is this?"

I was quickly becoming the leader of whatever this was and definitely the only one willing to tell Marcus. "We just ran into Joseph."

Marcus opened his mouth to say something. Ingrid cut him off. She stepped out from behind a dressing curtain where she'd been putting on her next outfit. "There's that name again. Who's Joseph?"

My jaw hit the ground as she appeared in flannel pyjamas. It wasn't the outfit that dropped my jaw, but the fact that she was here. Why wouldn't she be here? She was his model. Had Marcus ever told her about his past? "He's my old boss."

It wasn't a lie and Heidi added to it. "He's also my father." She extended her hand. "My name is Heidi. I'm an old friend. You look lovely. I get what Marcus sees in you."

Ingrid frowned. "Didn't I see you at the funeral?"

"I was there. I'm surprised you noticed."

"You're a cute girl, hard not to notice you. How is your father?"

"He's not doing as well as we'd like."

"Oh?"

"It's his heart. He needs a new one, but not to worry. Hopefully he'll find one some day."

"A heart?"

"Enough about him. You're a model and that is so exciting. What other outfits do you have?"

Ingrid looked over to Marcus for a second and then took Heidi's hand. She pulled her toward the curtain. "Come see. So what happened to you?"

"I broke my nose to get out of jury duty."

"Really?"

"No, but it beats the truth. I slipped in the tub washing my hair."

She told it with such conviction that I almost believed her. None of us said a word until they were out of earshot. Then Marcus put the camera down. "What the hell is going on here? And why is Heidi here?"

"Her father just about threw her off the Arc de Triomphe. He wants revenge."

"No," Eddy interrupted. "He wants us to steal something for him, something worth a small fortune."

"But we aren't thieves. Did you tell him to go to hell?"

"Couldn't. He'll come after us." I looked over to Ingrid and Heidi. "He wants the four of us to rot in jail. He'll use Ingrid for leverage if you say no. You know how this works."

Marcus nodded. "What does he want?"

Ingrid and Heidi were wearing Dior sunglasses when they returned. Ingrid put her hands up. "This girl is a real sweetheart. Where'd you find her?"

The three of us stood quiet. Heidi was a lot of things, but not one of us would have chose sweetheart. Words like manipulative, persuasive, tenacious, crafty and dangerous came to mind long before sweetheart ever would.

"I'm serious," Ingrid continued. "Did you know she's trying to work things out with her father? That's so incredible." She turned to Heidi. "He's family and you can't change that. I don't always get along with my own father. He's a very proud man."

"That's my Dad," Heidi half-boasted.

"Isn't it just like the men in our lives?" She looked over to Marcus and he returned a frown.

Heidi shrugged and put a hand on my shoulder. "We can't all be like this guy."

Marcus had heard enough. "We've got to get back to work."

I had to agree. These two women needed separation. ""I'll be in touch. Let's go, Heidi."

Marcus started rummaging through his bag for more film. "Sounds good."

Ingrid gave Heidi a hug and I could tell she was looking at the what-ifs. Could Jon rekindle something here? Would it be right?

I shot her a heavy dose of stink eye. "Stop doing that."

Chapter thirty six

I was dressed and had morning coffees ordered before eight. Room service brought them with a side of pancakes. I wasn't angry with her and there was no reason to treat her like Marcus and Eddy had. She didn't hear me answer the door. Instead she lay motionless, hidden under a stack of covers. She did however stir when the aroma of the coffee reached her.

"Morning. Did you get one for me?" she asked.

"Coffee and breakfast." I waited for her to sit up in bed. Then I handed her the plate and fork. When I set the coffee on the nightstand I noticed something that I hadn't seen since I first met her. It was innocence and it was a complete letdown of her guard.

"Extra syrup?" I asked.

The look she gave me reminded me of the first time I bought her long strings of black licorice. We spent more time tying knots in it than eating it. "Thank you."

I continued to get ready to go out. I had to comb my hair, brush my teeth and find a better shirt. I was hoping to find one with a few less wrinkles than the one I was wearing.

Heidi watched me dig through my things while she finished the first pancake and started on the second. "What are you looking for?"

"A shirt with no wrinkles."

"Steam one." She jumped out of bed, picked up one of the shirts along with a hanger and headed for the bathroom.

I heard the shower start up and peeked inside. The water was hot and the shirt was hanging on the far end of the shower curtain rod.

"Where are you going?" she asked.

"I have to go to Lawrence's office."

"Lawrence?" She tried to place the name.

"My brother."

"Oh ya. Georg is Lawrence, Rebecca's brother in-law." She got up and started routing through her suitcase. "I'm coming with you."

"No."

"Oh, hell yes. If you've got a brother, I want to meet him. He might as well be my family."

"I don't think this…"

She held up a silk blouse. "Is this dressy enough?" She dropped it down and lifted a knee length skirt. "And this?"

"I just wanted to…"

She ducked into the bathroom. Steam poured out from the open door. She dressed, turned off the water and exited the room with my shirt. The wrinkles were gone.

"Wrinkle-free. Now you owe me."

I looked at the shirt and couldn't find a wrinkle. It was like some kind of voodoo. "Okay, but no talking. He's my brother."

"Of course. You know me."

Thing is, I did know her. While we drove I continued to let her know that it was imperative that she kept quiet. It wasn't until we were walking up to his office that I let her know I was signing a business contract.

Lawrence eyed her from head to toe and smiled as he offered a couple of chairs in front of his desk. I felt an instant need to introduce her as a friend that was visiting from Germany.

"I've known Johannes since elementary school. He worked briefly for my father."

Lawrence's smile wilted. "So he's like a big brother?"

"Exactly."

I wanted to correct her. She was nothing like a sister, had always been a lot more than that. My mouth opened and she cut me off.

"It's so nice to meet you Lawrence. When I heard my Jon had a brother I was shocked. I had to meet you. I hope that's okay."

"I was pretty surprised myself," Lawrence replied. Then he pulled a stack of papers out of a folder. "Well Jon, are you ready for this?"

I looked around the office. From the new windows to the smell of fresh paint, this deal seemed right. I took the pen out of his hand and started to sign. I'm sure Heidi had a million questions, but she knew her place.

Lawrence picked up his phone and had his secretary bring a bottle of champagne and three glasses. She poured and we all touched glasses.

"To finding my brother," I toasted.

Lawrence took a sip. "And to a successful family business."

Heidi became the mouse in the corner. She sipped her wine, took in every word and studied Lawrence like there was going to be a test afterward. That scared me.

Then, out of the blue, the red haired teenager from before waltzed into the room. She came unannounced, which seemed odd to me. It also caught Lawrence off guard. He immediately got to his feet and excused himself.

He came back a minute later. "I wanted to take you out for lunch, Jon, but something's come up. Can I interest you and Heidi to go in my place? I had reservations at a pretty posh place a block away. I'd hate to let it go. My treat."

As much as I loved a free meal, I had a more pressing issue. "I'm sorry, Lawrence. I'm a little busy today. Maybe we can get together in a couple days."

Lawrence seemed surprised that someone might pass on a free meal. Still, he accepted my decision and walked us out.

Downstairs my quiet little mouse became a lion. "What did you just sign?"

"Lawrence and I just bought this building. We are partners in a property management company. Bet you never thought I'd be a business man."

"I still don't. What the hell do you know about property management?"

"Absolutely nothing. My brother, on the other hand, is a whiz."

"So what are you bringing to the table?"

"Our inheritance."

"No. Do not tell me you handed over all your money."

"Half of it was his."

"How do you figure? Was it willed to him?"

"Well no, but…"

"Now I don't like him."

"You don't even know him."

"I've know his kind all my life."

I shook my head as I started toward the Metro. "You just met him."

"He's a shyster. I've made it my mission to know people. Trust me on this one."

"He's my brother." I waited for her to catch up, but she wasn't moving. "Not a shyster. What's up?"

"The man can be a brother and a shyster." She started to walk in the other direction. "And I also have something to do."

"What?"

"If we're going to become art thieves, I need to concoct a plan. That means making a few phone calls and seeing what kind of contacts I have."

"I don't think we should split up."

"My people won't talk if you're around. You look like a narc."

"I don't look like a narc."

She dipped her head to the right and rolled her eyes.

I switched gears. "Should I go to the Louvre and find out where they keep that painting?"

"Couldn't hurt. Get a map and walk the place. I want to know where the painting is, where the cameras are, and how many steps to each exit. Put the numbers on the map. And see if the painting has sensors."

"Sensors?"

"Walk up to it and see how close you can get. My guess is that an alarm will sound if you get within eighteen inches of it. Also look for guards. Mark them on the map."

"Cameras, guards, seriously?"

"And look for alternate escape routes."

My jaw hung open.

"Air conditioning vents, widows large enough to break through, drains and sewer passages."

"Sewer passages?"

She smiled, but I knew she was serious.

Chapter thirty seven

It was only a two-block walk from the Metro as the rain began to fall. There was a closer stop, but I was looking for options. Everything was an obstacle for an art thief. You needed to have options, at least I think that's what Heidi was getting at. Could we get a painting wet? Would the colours run? How many blocks would we have to walk to get to our getaway car? Do crossing guards have the authority to make an arrest?

The rain made the cement around the glass pyramid of the Louvre's entrance look like ice. It was a postcard except for the mood that hung over the museum. In less than a day I'd be getting arrested. So would three of my friends, unless I could find a way to steal this damn painting.

Inside I was patted down by Security and allowed to take the escalator down to the main opening. I found a map of the museum abandoned on a bench and gave it a read through. I didn't find the painting.

There was a bookstore in the mall section of the museum. I picked up a coffee and went into the store to find a better map. Instead, I found a book of every picture, every statue, and every piece of art currently in here. There was the Sully Wing, which seemed fairly central, the Richelieu Wing on one side and the Denon Wing on the other. There were several sections in each on multiple floors and I couldn't believe the actual size of this place. It was a lot larger on the inside.

I eventually found the Café Terrace painting on the upper floor in the Richelieu Wing. It was over eight hundred steps from the nearest exit. Being up on the second floor there were no sewer drains and jumping out of one of the windows would have to be a last resort. I walked up to one of the windows and looked out. It had to be twenty feet to the sidewalk.

I paced my way to the stairs and looked for an air duct, extra exit door or a fireman's pole. There was nothing. My hope was depleting fast. Getting caught seemed to be the only option.

Remembering back to that day, I should have taken the fall for Joseph. I would have had a record, but it wouldn't have followed me. It wasn't like I was running for Chancellor of Germany. I'd have done a couple months, maybe, and then six months probation. Thing was, Heidi would have been beaten how many times in the last eleven years?

After looking down at the sidewalk and second-guessing actions of the past, I walked back to the painting. Why this one?

It was a scene from a Paris restaurant. There was an outdoor patio with tables and chairs. There were patrons enjoying the night ambience, and a shadow of a figure leaving to the left. The building was a blazing yellow with a night sky and stars that twinkled in a way that only Van Gogh could paint them. In the middle of it all was a man dressed in white. I stared at that man. Was he a waiter?

I moved in for a closer look. At two feet I could see the detail in the windows, the detail in the cobblestones. I got within a foot and the alarm went off. I jumped back and waited for the security officials to rush in and tackle me to the ground.

After a lengthy forty-five seconds a chubby man with a limp poked his head in the room.

"Can I get you to step back please?"

I took another step back. "I'm sorry. I didn't realise we weren't allowed to get that close."

"No problem. Middle of the day we know it's just someone having a better look." He pointed to the sign that asked people to stay back. "If it were after hours I'd have my gun out."

The man patted his hip, where the gun should have been, but wasn't. "What? We're not closed yet."

"What do they do to art thieves?"

"Depends. If we don't have to chase them it's five years. If they get down the street it's eight. It's twenty if we don't catch them until the next day."

"Crime doesn't pay."

"Not here it doesn't."

The man left and I did one last scan of the exits. During business hours there was no way out other than the main exits. After it closed there was no way out, but security was expected. So how would we get the painting off the wall, carry it eight hundred paces to the nearest exit and get it through a very solid and locked door.

The map was soon filled with numbers, scribbled sideways, upside down as well as exits and a big 'x' that marked the painting. I stuffed it in my pocket and headed for the main exit. This day had turned out to be a waste of time. All I'd accomplished was proving the obvious. This painting was safe.

Outside I needed to refocus. I left the Louvre and started walking toward the Eiffel Tower. I needed to think. No matter how many outcomes rolled through my head, the conclusion was the same. Somehow, I had to keep the others from getting caught. Joseph wasn't angry with his daughter anymore than he was angry with Eddy or Marcus.

It was me he wanted. It was me he'd get.

Chapter thirty eight

The first time I met Joseph I was six. He was the father of the girl who was helping me survive elementary school. Being painfully shy, I wasn't any good at making friends. She forced me to be her friend first and Marcus was quickly added. Eddy was eventually added in middle school. As teenagers, we were an odd and yet inseparable group of misfits.

And as teenagers we needed a means to make money. Getting into trouble at this age was a costly affair. While the lucky ones got jobs at the local supermarkets and shops, we relied on the generosity of Heidi's father. He was a businessman and although we didn't fully understand why he wasn't delivering these packages, the money was good. In hindsight, we could have asked.

We had a pretty good idea what we were delivering after being told of the importance of not losing the packages. We never did. On a few occasions the drop was awkwardly done on our end and Heidi usually bore the brunt of our unprofessional encounters. I never connected the dots until much later when we started dating and she started sharing. After that, we were always on point with these deliveries.

And then there was the day everything went south. I'd never seen so many police. There had been multiple packages and the people we were delivering to were late. Heidi made the call to abort the drop and take everything back to her place. I initially said no. We'd never had these packages in our homes. It was always a pick up from an old trash bin behind the abandoned warehouse and a drop in a neutral area, like a parking lot, a park, or a quiet back alley. And it was always a package for a package. She assured me it would be fine.

At Heidi's place we waited for her father. She decided to make grilled cheese sandwiches, to calm the mood. When she was at ease, we all were at ease. When she was scared, we were terrified. She was our barometer letting us know in advance how everything would turn out. I, for one, trusted her.

When her father came home, he was in good spirits. He took one of the sandwiches and ate it while she told him about her science paper on clouds. His interest in her was as fatherly as it got. I looked over at the packages a few times and waited for her to bring them up, but she never did.

Then Joseph reached into his pocket and pulled out a box. "Think your Gramma might like this? Her birthday is coming up."

Heidi took it and opened the box. It was a strand of pearls. "They're beautiful. She'll love them."

"Did you make the drop?"

Heidi couldn't take her eyes off the pearls. "I have a birthday in two weeks."

"The drop. Did it go okay?"

She briefly looked over at the packages and that was when I noticed it. It was the first crack in her armour. Suddenly she was confused, concerned. "About that..."

Her words were cut short by the faint whining of sirens. Distant at first, they rapidly grew louder.

Joseph walked over to the window. "What the hell?"

I fought to hold my bladder as the sirens closed in on us. Marcus and Eddy didn't hesitate to run. They were out the back door, through the back yard and hopping the fence before I could register what they were up to. I was about to follow them when I heard Joseph yell.

He had grabbed Heidi's arm. "What happened today?"

"They didn't show."

"What?" He started to shake her. "What did you do with the packages?"

I wanted to save her but froze. Outside the sirens had stopped. His first blow landed against her face, a backhand that caught her just below the right eye. An open hand caught the side of her head and she staggered to the floor. "Get rid of them."

When she didn't move, he kicked her hard in the ribs. "Move it."

I continued to stare in horror. I'd always seen the aftermath of the bruises, never seeing how she got them. The man was a savage. It snapped me out of my trance. I lunged at him and pinned him against the wall. My right arm was around his throat and I was squeezing for all it was worth when the police broke in.

Heidi got up and tried to pull me off him. "No, Jon. He's not worth it."

She tugged at my arm, but I didn't let go until one of the police officers muscled us to the floor. Seconds later we were all face down on the carpet with our hands behind our backs. The police dragged us into different rooms where we were questioned.

I found out later that Joseph's story was that he'd found out his little girl was having sex with me and that was why he was angry. He felt bad about hitting her. He also said he had no idea where those packages had come from.

Heidi just cried and played the part of the victim.

"Who do the packages belong to, kid?"

I looked up at the two officers with the blankest of expressions. All I could think about was him hitting her, kicking her. How many times had I seen the bruises, a split lip, black eye, blackened wrists or the darkened skin around her neck? It had always bothered me and she had always passed it off as no big deal. She'd always remind me of the bruises I got playing football. It wasn't much different. Maybe I didn't want to deal with it, or maybe I wasn't sure how, but I let her talk me out of it being a big deal.

But it was a big deal. I had just seen him hit her with a strong swing of his arm. When she was down he had kicked her hard enough to lift her off the floor. On any other day, I'd have seen those bruises and she'd have shrugged them off…no big deal.

"Hey, kid. I asked you a question."

"I want to see if she's okay."

"You can see her later. Who do the packages belong to?"

I tried to push the image of her bruises out of my mind. I didn't want to see them, couldn't see them. How could I do what needed to be done? And how could I keep telling myself she'd be okay if I wasn't here? I tried one last time to push them away and couldn't.

"They belong to her Dad."

I continued to walk toward the Eiffel Tower until I saw her sitting at a bench. My heart stopped and I swear my tongue swelled to twice its size. At least it felt twice the size when I opened my mouth to talk.

"Madeline? It's nice to see you, again."

Chapter thirty nine

Madeline quickly got to her feet and let me slip my arms around her. She smelled amazingly familiar. It made my heart flutter so I gave her peck on each cheek. I'm not sure what I was thinking, or maybe I wasn't thinking. Waves of stupid were washing over me like they had back at the apartment.

"Hi, Johannes," she said softly.

"You can call me Jon. I know you prefer it."

I let the hug continue longer than it should have, but she wasn't fighting to get away. I simply closed my eyes and let her become my Rebecca. I tried to ignore these feelings, but this was stronger than logic.

When the hug was over she became Madeline again. "Please sit back down."

She briefly took my hand and sat back on the bench. I took the spot beside her, sitting close enough for our hips to touch. Why had she taken my hand?

"How amazing is this," I started my lie. "I was walking from the train, looking for a place to get a bite to eat, and something told me to walk through the park."

"That is pretty amazing, Jon."

"Hey, I'm sorry about the weirdness a week ago. Ingrid talked to me about that."

"No. I think I was being overly snotty that day." She put her hand on my knee. "I know I look a lot like her. Sometimes I forget."

The touching rattled me. "Still, I don't know you as well as I knew your sister and I seem to forget that when I see you."

"Really, it's okay."

She kept strong eye contact, and was that a flirtatious grin? God she looked like Rebecca. I could see it in her eyes, in her smile and in each little hand gesture. I took a deep breath and let it out slowly. "I want to thank you again for dinner the other night. It was amazing, a life changer. Isn't Lawrence a great guy?"

"He's, uh, good."

An awkward silence fell over us like a wet blanket. I think she felt it as much as I did. We never knew each other all that well. The only thing we had in common was Rebecca.

She slowly got to her feet. "It's nice to see you, but I should get going."

"What's wrong, Madeline?"

"Nothing. I'm just a little tired. Lawrence told me you two had a meeting yesterday."

"Yes, about that." I stood up, reached into my pocket and pulled a folded piece of paper out of my pocket. She unfolded the paper to see a copy of Lawrence's original birth certificate. The man really was a Georg before becoming a Lawrence.

"He's my brother, Madeline, or should I call you sister."

She cringed and I could tell she was forcing a smile. What was going on in that head of hers? "He's working on an investment strategy."

"Are you sure about all this?"

"Don't worry, Madeline. I've got a good feeling about this." But for the first time I was concerned. It was like she knew something. "Why do you ask?"

Her mood turned to melancholy. "No reason."

No reason, except her nothing was something. I decided to let it go. "Has Nicolas been enjoying his bedtime stories?"

Her eyes lit back up. "Nicolas doesn't let that book out of his sight when we're at home."

Nicolas came over and tugged on her pant leg. "Wet."

"Yes you are. Are you done playing?" she asked.

"Duckies gone."

"Those silly duckies." She started to dry him off. "Nicolas, do you remember Johannes?"

Nicolas jumped to attention and offered me a very rigid hand to shake. It melted me so I shook his little hand with a very adult shake. "Wow, you have a very strong grip."

Nicolas pulled up his sleeve and made a muscle. I gave it a squeeze and nodded my approval. Madeline slipped a wet shirt off and a dry one on.

"Now scoot the pants, mister," she demanded.

He shed the trousers and as soon as the underwear came off, he started to run.

She got up and gave chase. "What possesses little boys to run around as soon as they're naked?"

I laughed while I ran. "It's just what we do."

We managed to corral him back to the bench. She got him dressed and combed his hair. "What is Marcus up to?"

That question surprised me. Did she know Marcus? Had she ever met him? "He's decided to take some time off. He and Ingrid can't handle any more clients. Rebecca and Ingrid gave his company quite a reputation. He's had to turn people away. They're getting burnt out."

She sat back down. Again she became silent.

"Madeline?" The voice came from behind us. "We meet again. How is my favourite person?"

She spun around and whispered something to him. I suddenly felt like a third wheel.

The man eyed me from head to foot. "Who is your friend, Maddie?"

"Ricardo, this is Johannes."

He held out a hand and I took it. He held it longer than he should. "And how do you know Madeline?"

I returned his stare with one of my own. "I used to date her sister."

He looked back at her stupefied. "You have a sister?"

"Yes. Her name was Rebecca," she answered. "Don't you have somewhere to be?"

"In my dreams, I am already there."

"You should probably go and take care of those dreams. I have no doubt you're good at that."

"I'm always around, Maddy. I will see you later."

Sensing the tension, I put a hand on his shoulder and ushered him away. "Nice to meet you, Ricardo."

She seemed relieved when I got rid of the man.

"He's quite a piece of work, Madeline. So how do you know him?"

"You wouldn't believe me if I told you."

I could tell that this was her way of saying it was none of my business. "Okay."

"Honestly, he's nobody."

I had already let it go. I had my own problems. "How are your parents?"

"Good. They'd love to see you."

"That would be nice." I wasn't kidding. I hadn't called them and let it go far too long. "I've always liked visiting them. They remind me of my parents."

"I could set something up. You're probably busy though."

"I do have a lot to do. I'm renovating my apartment, but I can always find time for them, and for you. I'm staying in a hotel." I handed her a card. It had my room number on it. "Please, don't be a stranger."

"Renovations?"

"The building had some electrical issues. I'm living at the hotel until I can get things fixed."

"I'll find a time that works for them."

"It was good seeing you again, Madeline." I gave her another hug. This time it was brief and awkward. Confusion danced in her eyes as it did in mine. Shaking the feeling, I started to walk away. I understood my confusion. What was hers?

"Good seeing you too, Jon."

"Bye, Madeline. Call me, sometime."

I thought about her as I left. Would she know how to get a hold of me in prison?

Chapter forty

I had the bed all to myself last night. Heidi had either found a better bed or she was in trouble. I generally believed that if there was trouble, it was her bringing it. Lately I wasn't as sure about that. The coffee had just arrived when the phone rang.

"Hello?" I answered.

"Hello, Jon. It's Madeline. So how are you doing today?"

I wanted to answer that I wasn't in prison yet. "Fine thanks. I'm surprised to hear from you so soon."

"I just got off the phone with my parents, just touching base with them, and I mentioned that I ran into you. They wanted to hear all about it and I remembered what you said about wanting to see them. If you're still interested, they can do lunch today."

"I have an appointment at eleven, but it shouldn't be more than an hour." That is if Marcus didn't kill me. "I could shoot for twelve-thirty if that works for you."

"That'll work."

The silence reached an uncomfortable length. "I'll see you around noonish?"

"Noonish sounds good."

I hung up and wasn't five minutes into my coffee when Heidi showed up. She came through the door like this was her place and sat on the edge of the bed. I took the chair by the desk.

"Good morning, Jon."

"Is it? You haven't told Marcus about our job offer, have you?"

"Nope. I'm guessing you called him?"

"He'll be meeting us at eleven." I offered her my coffee. "Where were you last night?"

"I was out devising a plan."

I tossed her my map. "My homework assignment."

She looked it over. "This works with what I have in mind."

"You mean to tell me you think we can pull this off?"

"Anything is possible if you're prepared."

"So I'm guessing you've also figured out a way to tell Marcus?"

"I shouldn't have to do it all."

And with that we left the room. Today I decided to take the car. The Metro would have got us around a lot quicker than the car, but I wanted the freedom to leave whenever I wanted. Driving also helped me think. Maybe it would help me figure out how I was going to tell him.

Marcus was waiting and, as asked, he was alone. Heidi and I took chairs across from him and waved the waitress over. "Two more coffees, please."

Marcus motioned for a refill. "What does Joseph want?"

I waited for Heidi to tell him. She waited me out.

"Come on," Marcus snapped. "What is it?"

This time he asked me directly. I initially looked down, but quickly raised my eyes back to his. "He wants a painting."

"And…"

"It's in the Louvre."

"Well that's impossible. How are we supposed to do that?"

I turned to Heidi because it was her turn to talk.

She seemed surprised to see the underside of the bus, more surprised to see me driving it. "Okay. I have a plan and although it's a bit of a long shot, it is possible."

"Will he take anything else, money or favour?"

"We can do this," Heidi admitted. "I've called in a few favours."

"What kind of favours?" he asked.

"I don't dare say. I'll know more in couple hours. We'll need to meet back here around three. I'll tell you everything you need to know in order to pull this off, and we will pull this off."

I pushed my coffee aside. I wasn't thirsty or hungry. "You say that like you mean it."

"I wouldn't be a part of this unless I did." She sat back in her chair. The smile was a smug one as she took a sip from her coffee. "And I am a part of this."

Marcus expected a response from me. It never came. All I could do was shrug.

He sat back. "If I see you there then I'm in. If any of you say a word of this to Ingrid I'll be out."

I got up to leave. Heidi got up to follow and I stopped her. "No. I need a break from all this. I'll see you back here at three."

Heidi didn't push and I didn't look back as I made my way to the car. She didn't have the same power over me with Madeline on my mind. I looked forward to seeing her again, seeing my Rebecca.

It only took twenty-five minutes to get to Rebecca's parent's apartment. I was a little worried about seeing them, but I needed to see her. I rang the buzzer and her father answered.

"Hello?"

I cleared my throat. "It's me, Johannes."

"I'll buzz you up, Johannes."

I took a couple minutes to climb the stairs and her father let me in. Madeline was standing behind him. I swallowed hard and held out my hand.

"Come in Jon." Mr Harrows dragged me into the house with a handshake. "Have a seat. Lunch is ready."

I sat across from Madeline. It was a good visit and the conversation had stayed light until I told them about Lawrence. Her father looked over at her, hurt that she hadn't mentioned anything. I could tell that her mother was also shocked. The idea of me being Lawrence's brother took a minute for them to register.

Her mother's soup and sandwiches hit the spot, but soon two hours had passed. I had to face my reality and meet up with Marcus, Eddy and Heidi.

"You want me to walk you down?" she asked.

"I should be able to find my way."

"I really don't mind. I can work off some of Mom's short rib soup."

"If you want to then." I started down the steps and she trailed closely behind in her stockinged feet. There was no further conversation until we had reached the bottom.

"So," I began. "We should get together for dinner some day."

Why had I said that? As if I hadn't created enough problems with Heidi, now I was throwing Rebecca's ghost into the mix. A part of me wished that I hadn't found my brother. Having him in my life meant having her in my life.

"That would be terrific." She saw me differently today, saw me in a way that reminded me of how I was seeing her. Her eyes were locked on mine. It was sweet.

"It's my turn. I can take you and Lawrence out on the town."

Suddenly, she looked like I had puked on her socks. I wanted to take back my offer, but that would have made things worse. With any luck she'd simply say no.

"Yes, that would be best."

Her sudden indifference confused me. "Did I say something wrong? We don't need to…"

"No, I just have to check his calendar. He's a busy man."

"Oh, that's okay. I can check with him."

"I suppose you can." We continued out to the sidewalk and she gave me a very sisterly hug. Again, she left me wondering after the more interesting hugs from yesterday. I drove around the corner and stopped. I had to compose myself before seeing Heidi.

That woman could see right through me.

Chapter forty one

I heard the knocking on the door, but couldn't comprehend where I was, or what time it was. After Heidi had started sharing her plan, I had started drinking. The more she talked, the more I drank. Soon my wallet was empty and she was driving my car. I remember her tucking me into bed. Did she sleep here last night? She wasn't here now.

I got to my feet when the knocking started up again. I was already in my jeans, but had to throw on a shirt. Heidi's suitcase was still here, closed, and stuffed under the desk.

The knocking persisted and I wondered if Heidi was bringing coffees. I unlocked the door and opened it to see two police officers.

"Can I help you?"

He looked past me. "We're looking for a Heidi Dietrich."

"I can't say I've seen her."

"But she is staying here?"

"I haven't seen her in days."

He stepped past me and took a look around. The other walked into the bathroom. Less than a minute later they took my name and quietly left. A sick feeling was settling in my stomach.

I picked up the phone and ordered a coffee, extra strong. My head was not only swimming in last night's alcohol, but in the news that the police were already looking for her, for us.

Sticking out from beneath the bed was a sock. It wasn't a man's sock and I was lucky the police didn't see it. They'd have torn the room apart and brought me in for questioning for sure. They'd have found her suitcase.

I picked up the sock and stuffed it in her suitcase, along with anything else she'd left out. And how many years would you get for conspiring to steal something? That was when I saw the folded paper under one of her shirts. It was older, worn. I unfolded it to see a picture. It was a photocopy of Van Gogh's painting, Terrace at Night. What was she up to?

A knocking on the door had my heart beating harder than it already was. The police had returned.

I was coming up with my story when I opened the door. It was room service with my coffee. She handed it over to me and closed the door. I needed to get a handle on this. More so, I needed to find Heidi and let her know they were on to her. Maybe her father had made an anonymous phone call. Maybe one of her allies betrayed her. Either way, she was slipping up and if she fell, we all fell. And why was there an old photocopy of the painting in her suitcase?

I picked up the phone and hesitated for a second before dialling.

There was an eerie silence when it was picked up. I waited through it for a minute. "Madeline, is that you? Can we talk?"

The silence continued.

"Madeline? Are you there?" I persisted because I needed my fix. "Madeline?"

"I'm here. Sorry, I was just juggling, uh, Nicolas's bottle."

The boy was close to two years old. "He's still on the bottle?"

"Pop! I mean he grabbed it out of the fridge and I was getting it away from him. It's a little, um, early…shit."

That made me chuckle.

"What did you call for?"

"It was nice seeing your parents. I had talked to Ingrid a couple days ago. She told me how you're struggling with memories. I know we haven't talked much about that. I'm also struggling with a few."

"The accident made my brain a bit of a clean slate."

"If I can help…I mean if you need to talk…"

"Thank you."

"The reason I called is because I've always felt bad about something. I never got to see you or your parents after Rebecca died."

"I heard you missed Rebecca's funeral." She paused. "I mean I heard you didn't go."

"I would have gone, but it was a terrible time. You don't need the details, but I had received a phone call only minutes before talking to your Dad. It was from the hospital in Frankfurt. We'd had snow and the roads were dangerous. It was my parents."

"What happened, Johannes?"

"They were returning from Rüdesheim when their car slid off the road and into the Rhine River. I'm sure Dad had a couple glasses too many. People tried to get them out of the frigid water, but they were too late."

"I'm so sorry, Jon."

I was happy she understood. "I felt guilty missing Rebecca's funeral. I meant to call, but what could I have said to them? Soon I had let it go too long. How could I call them and dredge up such horrific feelings? Then I found out about my brother. Finding him was such a good distraction that I thought I had healed. But seeing you has brought her back."

"Oh Jon."

"I'm sorry. This must be hard for you."

"Yes, but I don't mind talking about her. Oddly it keeps her alive."

"I'm glad."

"It feels like years, doesn't it?" she asked.

"It does." I found myself sweating. "There are days when time has stalled. Life is not the same without her. Again, I just wanted to call and tell you how sorry I was about your sister. She was an incredible soul and the world won't be the same without her. Maybe we can do lunch sometime. I enjoy talking about her."

"I would like that." She paused as if the idea brought possibilities. "I have to run, Jon."

There was a click and with it, our connection to the past was gone.

Chapter forty two

The morning coffee worked at clearing my head, while the conversation I'd just had worked at clouding it back up again. She had wanted to do a lunch. Maybe I had read too much into it, or maybe she was as curious as I was. Either way, she had wormed her way into my brain in a manner that I shouldn't have allowed.

What I could allow was a change of thought. When the phone rang, I answered it on the first ring. "Hello?"

"It's Eddy. How are you feeling? You drank enough for all of us."

"Considering I'll be robbing the Louvre in a few hours, I feel pretty damn good."

"Do you think her plan might work?" he asked.

"No."

"Then maybe we should try my plan."

"If you've got a plan? I'm all ears."

"We know where the exits are. I say we find them sooner than later when shit hits the fan."

"I can't leave her that way."

"Come on, Jon. Be smart. We'll never get out of there without being caught and thrown in jail. It's the bloody Louvre. We'll rot in prison, just like her damn father wants. I'll do what she asks of me to get things started, but then Marcus and I are out and gone. I've talked to Marcus and he says he'll do the same if you do too. Are you in?"

I thought about the photocopy of the painting for a second and knew they'd be better off if they ran. They couldn't know about what I'd found or they wouldn't show up.

"Okay. I'll run on the first alarm. Tell Marcus to do the same."

"I will. Where do you want to meet?"

"Not my hotel. The police just dropped by looking for Heidi."

"Shit. All the more reason for us to run when we get the chance."

I agreed, although I'd have a hard time leaving her.

"Where is she? I thought she was staying with you."

"She was gone when I woke up. No note and I don't imagine we'll see her again until six." The more I thought about it the more I knew she had to be playing us and her father was behind this. "Hey, when we make our escape we should meet at the park behind Notre Dame. It's close and we can take off in about four different directions if the police come after us."

"Sounds good," Eddy agreed. "See you at six."

"See you then."

I had just set the phone down when it rang again. It was Madeline. "Hey, it's me. Is there any chance we can do lunch today?"

This would be my last supper and I had to have one last look at her. "Of course. You know I always enjoy the company of you and Nicolas. When?"

"Can I pick you up in say, half an hour?"

I sensed urgency. "Sounds serious. Is everything okay?"

"Everything's good."

"See you in half an hour then."

I hung up and started the shower. If I did go to prison, I'd want to be clean. Only God and criminals knew what prison showers looked like.

The shower I took was a long one. It helped me think. Heidi had a plan and I would have been okay following it through if it weren't for that damn paper. I'm glad that Eddy and Marcus wanted to run. Neither of them deserved this, and I hoped I could do the same when the time came. How could I let her take the fall for the three of us? Maybe I could get her out and take the fall on my own. That way it would be over. My rotting in jail was what Joseph wanted.

I had an inheritance and it was now with my brother. By the time I got out of jail I'd be twice as wealthy. I could purge this life in order to make room for a new one. A new life might not be so bad.

I was out of the shower and dressing when a knocking on the door froze me. Was it the police again, Heidi?

When the door opened, Madeline and Nicolas barged their way past me.

"I'm sorry. Can Nicolas use your bathroom?"

I pointed to a door on the other side of an unmade bed. "Definitely."

She got Nicolas settled.

I was buttoning up my shirt when she returned from the bathroom. "Sorry again, Johannes. How are you?"

"I'm good." I held my arms out for an innocent hug.

Her arms made their way around my waist. I could feel her fingers lightly caressing every contour of my body. This hug was more than a simple hello and it lasted far too long. My ghost was back.

I knew it was wrong, but couldn't contain myself. It was as comforting as a child's blanket, and damn if I didn't deserve this. I hadn't been held like this since...

She continued to hold me. I opened my eyes and looked down to see her staring up at me. Her eyes were trying to read mine, wanting me to take a chance. Should I roll the dice and accept the outcome?

My lips met hers. I closed my eyes and let her become my Rebecca. She kissed me like my Rebecca always did. My heart pounded as she mashed her body against my chest. Her nails dug into my back as her tongue swirled and darted around mine.

I pushed her away. "What are we doing?"

Her expression went blank. "I'm sorry. This was my fault."

"Mine too. I shouldn't have done this, but you're so damned intoxicating."

"Don't make it into something terrible, Jon. I see what my sister saw in you. You're a kind and amazing man."

I couldn't look away, more afraid than sorry. I had wanted more and I felt horrible for that.

Nicolas emerged from the bathroom and Madeline laughed.

"What's so funny?" I asked.

"My chaperone is definitely not getting his ice cream today." She saw the confusion in my eyes. "Why do you think I always keep him close when you're around? I can't trust myself."

"I think lunch is a bad idea."

"This is my fault, Jon. I'm an adult and I know better."

"Is there something wrong with you and Lawrence?"

"I can't talk about it. Let's say that Lawrence and I aren't what everybody thinks. He's your brother, so I won't get into it. He has his world and I'm just a wife living in it."

"What are you saying?"

"My husband, my problem." She gave me a half-cocked smile.

"You look so much like her, the way she smiles, the way she scrunches her nose when she thinks. It plays on me, makes me believe you are her. I swear I see her in your eyes. Is that crazy?"

"It's not that crazy, and I should leave." She pulled a slip of paper out of her pocket. "I honestly came over because I still don't like the fact that Lawrence is handling your money. I have no reason to believe he's out to get you, but it's all your inheritance and I worry. I found this in the trash. Do you have anybody that could decipher it?"

"There's a guy who was helping me find Georg, I mean Lawrence. He's a whiz with this stuff. I'm not so good at it. That's why I don't mind Lawrence handling our money." I couldn't tell her my guy was Heidi. "Madeline, I'm sorry about the kiss."

"We all know your brother was never my best choice. Keep me posted on the note."

I watched her leave while her kiss still tingled on my lips. Maybe Eddy and Marcus's plan wasn't so bad.

Chapter forty three

We all took our positions behind the counter full of aged Turkish tiles while the voice on the PA system announced the Louvre was now closed. It was different from the earlier warnings, which kindly asked people to complete their purchases before making their way to the main exit. This one was abrupt, like it was talking to the disrespectful dawdlers, the pretentious art connoisseurs, and the troublesome art thieves.

"We're gonna get caught," Eddy whispered.

"We're not getting caught." Heidi snapped. She said it with so much conviction that I actually believed her. "But change of plans on our jobs."

"What?" I asked.

"You're with me, Jon. I need you to carry the painting out. Eddy, you need to take care of the cameras."

"How do I do that?"

"You remember where the electrical room is, right?"

"Yes, three doors down the hall on the right."

"There's a room full of monitors just two doors farther on the same side. There's going to be a guard come through this room in about five minutes. He's doing a walkthrough to make sure there are no stragglers. I need you to follow him out. When he goes in the monitor room, you go in the electrical room. There are three panels on the right. You want the middle one."

"What am I doing with it?"

"You'll be killing the lights in here. That'll be our cue to get moving. You'll also be killing the cameras."

"How do I do this?"

"Kick three breakers off. You'll want breakers twenty-nine, sixty-four and one twenty-two. That's in the middle panel."

Marcus shook his head. "Won't the electrical room be locked?"

Heidi pulled a brand new key out of her pocket and handed it to Eddy. "I owe a few favours on that key so don't lose it."

Not that I wanted to shoot any holes in her plan, but I also had a question. "The guard comes through, won't the guy in the control room see us hiding from him?"

"First of all, we're hiding in one of the camera's blind spots. There are several. Secondly, cutbacks have left these guys short-staffed. Companies make more money when they don't pay out as much in wages. He has to do the walkthroughs and man the cameras. There are three other guys, but two will go on break after they walk through their wings and the last one needs to lock the main entrance. He's on the far side."

Eddy put the key in his pocket. "Isn't he gonna kick the breakers back on?"

"Yes, so get out of there as soon as you kick the breakers off. It'll confuse him and buy us some time. There's a door right across from the electrical room. It's a maintenance room, mops, buckets and brooms. Hide out in there until you can get away. Then get your ass to the main exit. Tell them you were taking a crap."

"Then I'm free to go?"

"You wish," she said. "I need you to get in a blue Fiat. It'll be parked on Rue de Rivoli, unlocked and keys up in the visor. Get in it and stay put. You'll be our getaway driver."

"What do I do?" Marcus asked.

"You still need to trip those three paintings in the Denon wing. Remember, just trip them and get the hell out of there. The fire exit that we talked about on the main floor will allow you to get out of the building. It's a designated emergency escape."

"And it won't be locked?"

"It will. Trip a fire alarm, there's one by that door. Exits cannot be locked on the inside while the alarm is going off. It's a liability thing. Imagine visitors burning up on the wrong side of the door. Once you're out, run left and circle the block until you make your way to the Fiat."

"Won't the cameras be back on line? They'll see me."

"Not a chance. That computer takes a good twenty minutes to reboot. That being said, you'll be tripping alarms and they all have beepers that give them the section where the alarm was set off. There'll be at three guards there in less than a minute. And don't move the paintings. Just touch them."

"Why those three?"

"Complacency. I was in here earlier and set the one we're stealing off four times today. Each time the guard came and checked it out. I'm sure these guys were warned that there's some kind of glitch in the sensor's wiring. The three that you touch are on the other side of the building. They haven't been setting off alarms. I want all the security on that side."

There was a click and a door opened. We all remained quiet while the guard made his way into the room and around the exhibits. We had to move around our exhibit while he scoped out our side of the room. It reminded me of a game of hide and go seek, only with much higher stakes. Eventually he made his way to the far door and out of the room.

Heidi gave Eddy a tap on the shoulder. "That's you cue."

"And he isn't going to review the footage of when he was doing his walk-through?"

"He gets paid a shit wage to work a graveyard shift. Would you?"

Eddy shrugged. "You're right."

We watched Eddy make his way to the door and look back at us. I nodded, letting him know that our plan hadn't changed. Get out when the shit hit the fan. He slipped out, and followed the guard. The three of us stepped out from behind our hiding spot.

"One more thing, Marcus. Are you wearing a watch?"

He held his arm out. "Why?"

"There's a TV box in the back of the Fiat. When the alarm goes off, we're going to be seven to eight minutes before we're outside. I need you to grab the box and head over to the nearest door on that side of the building. I think the door is right across the street from it. Just be ready because I don't want to be running around with a painting. A new TV is a lot less conspicuous."

"And you want me there around..."

The lights suddenly went out.

"About eight minutes from now." She started for the door.

Marcus looked over to me and I nodded. He wouldn't be anywhere near that Fiat.

Chapter forty four

Heidi dragged me upstairs. She took the steps two at a time as we made our way to the corridors of the Richelieu wing. She headed left at the top of the stairs and I was on her heels. I couldn't believe we were actually doing this. My heart raced, my eyes were darting left and right, looking for guards that were on their way to the ringing alarm on the other side of the building. These guys would have been making their way to that section as fast as possible and would have knocked us over versus asking us why we were still here.

"It's this way," she said, slightly out of breath.

I remained right behind her as we went through section after section. "Is this alarm going off outside?"

"No, but you can be sure there's a bell ringing at the police station. During opening hours it doesn't. The police should be waiting for a phone call. They'll wait forty-five seconds. By then these guys should be telling them the paintings are okay."

The painting we wanted was right up ahead. It wasn't a big painting. That didn't make it worth any less. I reached for it and she shoved me back.

"No!"

"What? I thought we wanted this one."

"We do. We just have to wait for them to call the police first. When the alarm stops, we'll know they've made the call. Then we can trip this one. This one has glitched a few times already, remember, so I'm hoping they'll make the call right away. It'll buy us some time."

"When did you learn all this?"

"Let's just say I'm in good with all the right people."

We waited what seemed like forever for the alarm to stop. It was actually twenty-one seconds. At that point she gave me a head nod.

I grabbed the painting and gave it a tug. It didn't come right away, but the alarm sounded. Heidi looked in behind the painting, took out a pair of side cutters and cut an anchor wire. The painting came free.

"I'm glad you had those."

"Always prepared." She motioned with a head nod to go the way we came. She led while I carried the painting.

Her hand went up at the top of the stairs. I stopped. Then she pointed for a doorway. The one that we'd just passed. "Quick. A guard is coming."

It bothered her. He had obviously not been privy to our plan. He should have been at the other end of the Louvre with the others. We ducked into a room full of Rembrandts.

The guard took the stairs, rounded the corner and ran right past us. He didn't look in the doorway or even slow down when he started through the corridor. As soon as he passed, Heidi ushered me out and down the stairs. We hurried down them and quietly made out way to the exit. As we reached the door she checked her watch. "Shit."

"What?"

"We're too quick. It's only been six minutes."

"Don't worry about it." I dropped my head.

"Eddy's not going to be on the other side, is he?"

"He and Marcus took off." I pulled the paper out of my pocket.

"You hung around. Why?"

"I'm an idiot? I've known you too long. I couldn't let you go through this alone."

She surprised me with a kiss on the cheek. I thought she would have stuffed a fist in my eye. "You're not angry?"

"I would have liked a heads-up, but this works too." She tripped the alarm and shoved me through the door. "Run. The police will be coming with or without their phone call now. It's a second alarm. We'll have a dozen cop cars here within minutes."

I looked toward the car. Soon I saw the back of her running toward it.

"I'll get the key." She dove in the driver's side and flipped the visor down. The key fell to the floor. "Shit."

I tried to stuff the painting in the back but couldn't find the door latch. It quickly found a home in the back seat.

"Careful with that thing."

"Just drive."

She was still doubled over trying to find the key.

"Where the hell is the key?" I asked.

"It dropped to the floor."

I looked down as I heard the sirens. "Hurry!"

"Shut up and help me find it!"

The key wasn't around her feet because it had fallen on my side. I picked it up, shoved it in the ignition and turned it. The car lurched forward, causing her to stomp the clutch. "What are you doing, Jon?"

"I was starting the car."

"It's a frigg'n standard."

"My bad. Now let's get the hell out of here."

While the police cars started to fill the streets around the Louvre, we were driving down the road four blocks away.

"Look behind us," she asked. "Do you see anything?"

I quickly did a shoulder check. "Slow down. We're clear."

She looked back expecting a string of police cars to come flooding out of one the back alleys like rats smelling cheese. There were none.

I looked to her and laughed. "This can't be happening. We actually have a painting."

"We do, but don't get excited. We still have to get it to my father."

"Shouldn't he be pleased?"

"You would think, but this is my father, remember?"

I did.

Chapter forty five

J oseph was sitting in the passenger side of a newer Volkswagen van. It was a newer model that one of his boys had likely brought from Germany. They'd be expected to bring the painting back in it while he flew. That was the way he operated.

We pulled into a parking lot by the St. Denis Metro. It wasn't more than a spot to double-park without holding up traffic. We nosed the car up to Joseph's van. In the distance sirens wailed, but they weren't for us.

"Stay here, Jon," Heidi ordered. "If I give you the signal to get the hell out of here, then drive. Drive hard and don't let him catch you."

I had to ask. "Why do I need a signal?"

"Because I know he prefers you to rot in jail." She got out of the car. "Give me a second."

She walked up to the passenger side and her father rolled down the window. They talked for about five minutes before she came back.

"I've talked him into taking the painting."

"Good enough," I said. "Let's give him the damn thing and get out of here. I need a beer."

I got out of the car, slipped the painting into the empty cardboard box and walked it over to the side door. When it opened I handed it over. The man inside held it up to show his boss.

"Go to the car, Jon," Heidi snapped.

"What the hell…"

"Go to the car, Jon!"

"Not so fast." Joseph started to get out. I was in his sights. "I'm not done with this one."

"Go, Jon." Heidi pushed the door shut on her father. "The deal was a painting for his freedom. You have the painting. There will be no more negotiating."

"Maybe I don't want the painting anymore."

I started to back away. This was exactly what Heidi was worried about. He didn't want the painting anymore than he wanted Eddy or Marcus. They weren't the ones that should have taken the rap for him. Again Joseph tried to get out of the van and this time he shoved her aside.

Just then, four police cars pulled into the lot, lights flashing but no sirens. The officer in charge stepped out of one of the cars and came over. The others drew their guns. "Lose your way Mr Deitrich."

Heidi's father narrowed his eyes to angry slits. "How can I help you?"

"What do you have in the box?"

"That's not mine. These two are the ones you should be asking."

"Oh, we'll be talking to them as well." He motioned for two of the officers to handcuff us and put us in the back of one of the cars. Then he refocused on Joseph. "I'd like to see the registration for this vehicle."

Joseph got the driver to pull the papers.

The officer looked the papers over. "The box is in your van, Mr Deitrich."

"It is, but…"

He turned to his men. "Arrest them all for possession of stolen property."

"This isn't my painting."

"I know, yet it is in your van. Do you know we consider our artwork a national treasure?"

"What?"

"You did not steal from the Louvre or from the city of Paris. You stole from France. This is a very serious offence."

"You can't prove anything."

"Possession is all the proof we need."

The police cuffed and loaded Joseph and his men into the remaining cars. The painting was put in the trunk as evidence. Heidi and I sat alone in the back seat while the lieutenant gave his men their orders.

"Shouldn't they be a little more careful with that painting?" I asked.

Heidi shrugged. "Why? It's a forgery."

"What?"

"She looked at me, studying my reaction. "You are so damn innocent, it's sweet. This couldn't have worked out better. You know Heidi always gets what Heidi wants."

I couldn't argue that. "So what did we steal?"

"We all had roles to play in a sting. The Stuttgart police do not want drugs in their city, but you cannot stop the inevitable. The best they can hope for is a drug dealer with scruples. I have proven that I have them. When I took over my father's business I immediately had a meeting with the Commissioner. I explain my needs, to make money and employ criminals, and he explained his, limited sales to adults only and no violence. Neither of us have crossed that line."

"You brokered a deal with the police?"

"I did. They cannot stop crime, but manageable crime is acceptable. My Dad did not believe in that. He always wanted to grow the business, harder drugs, larger moves, and he never would have worked with the police. To him they were the enemy."

"But not with you. So what was this?"

"I worked out a deal with the Stuttgart police to set up a sting. I knew if could lure my father to Paris, I could get him to want this painting. He saw it in prison three years ago, this lovely patio scene at a bistro in Paris. It was all he ever talked about. When I suggested a 'win win' he took the bait."

"Win win?"

"If he gets the painting he wins. If you get arrested, he wins. Who doesn't like odds like that?"

"Was stealing the painting real?"

"Hell no. Stuttgart police were working with Paris police. They would never trust us with the real painting. There were plain-clothes cops everywhere. You just didn't see them. No, this painting is a forgery, but as far as my Dad's trial is concerned, the real one will be used for evidence. To everyone concerned, we stole the real painting. Only a select few will know better. Don't tell Marcus or Eddy it was a fake. They can never know."

"But the key, the cameras, the guards."

"The cameras never went down, and the key was given to me by the Curator of the Louvre. I'm sure the locks have already been changed. Two of those breakers were for the washrooms, the third for the lunch counter. Oh, and those weren't Louvre guards. Those guys were highly trained military men. They were also acting. Did you really think it would be that easy to steal from the Louvre?"

"No." But I did. I honestly thought we'd pulled it off.

The Lieutenant took us to the station, debriefed us as to what our story would be. Joseph's men robbed the Louvre with our help. A car chase ensued and they were quickly apprehended thanks to us. The media would be given that story and Heidi and our names would not be given. If anybody asked, we were working with the French Government. The heist would make the national news.

A squad car dropped us off at the hotel. I watched it pull away and sighed. "That was exciting."

"Yes, and now it's over." Heidi wiped at a tear that was rolling down her cheek.

Chapter forty six

T he tear came from the fact that she would be going back to Germany. My life was here, and hers was there. She'd go back to running her father's business and making Danny her right arm. I'd go back to apartment renovations and getting to know my brother. For that reason I let her drink wine and flirt the night away. We slept together and the girl was still dressed when we woke up. She was the new Heidi.

Curled up against me, she snuggled in closer. "Thanks for last night."

I put my arm around her and gave her a hug. I had thought about giving in to her. It would have taken my mind off Madeline. I was glad I didn't. And why had I kissed Madeline? I was thinking of telling Lawrence. Instead I decided to tell Heidi. "I kissed Madeline."

Heidi spun around to face me. "Your sister-in-law? Why would you do that?"

"She looks so much like Rebecca."

"Still. You can't do that again, Jon. She's Lawrence's wife. He's your brother."

"I know. Should I tell him?"

"No. I don't know how to say this, but Rebecca is gone. You won't find her in Madeline. She may look identical, talk identical and dress the same, but she doesn't have the memories you and Rebecca had. It wasn't her on those first dates or lying in each other's arms while the rain pelted against your bedroom window."

"How did you know we watched the rain on the window?"

"You're a dumb romantic. It was an easy assumption."

I gave her a kiss on the forehead, above the right racoon eye. "Look at you, drug queen getting all sentimental and wise."

"I may have burnt my father, and taken over his business, but I still have feelings. You know that, right?"

"I do and I'm glad. Don't ever lose that part of you."

"Not to worry."

The phone rang and I answered it. "It's for you."

"Police?"

I handed it to her. "Dunno."

She listened for a second before hanging up. "It was my guy. He's been finding some interesting activity on your new company. You might want to go talk to your new brother about it."

After she filled me in I got up and started to change. "Do you want to come along?"

"Nope. I'm going to nurse a hangover, order room service and then get up and get some fresh air. I need to get back to Germany, but not until tomorrow. Is that okay?"

"You're always welcome." I slipped on my shoes and headed out the door. "See you later?"

"At some point, I'm sure."

The drive took twenty minutes. It was Saturday and the traffic was a little heavier than normal. I pulled into the driveway and made my way to the door, but when I knocked, I heard moaning.

"Madeline? Is everything okay?"

The deadbolt clicked and I pushed the door open. She was falling and I caught her and quickly dragged her over to a chair by the table. She was all bloodied. "What the hell happened to you? Did somebody break in? I'm going to call the police."

"Don't. He took Nicolas."

"Who?"

"Lawrence."

"Lawrence did this? Was this about the kiss?"

"He doesn't know about that. He has my son."

"But…"

"He's nothing like you… Actually, you really should go. He could come back. I'll be fine."

I took a wet napkin and placed it on her cheek. "Does he do this often?"

"What made you come here?"

"I hoped to talk to Lawrence, but that's not important now."

She rolled her jaw and neck around, working the kinks out. She kept blinking, no doubt trying to clear her head. "How bad do I look?"

"I think you need stitches." I put my arm around her. "I'll get you to a hospital. Can you walk?"

"You really shouldn't get involved. He's your brother."

"A man that could do this is not my brother." I walked her to my car and took her to the hospital where they patched her up. It all seemed so efficient, like she'd done this so many times before. The lady behind the counter filled out her form without asking the usual questions or what had happened to her. She already had her answers.

"What's going on Madeline? They all act like they know you."

"It's happened before."

"And what is this? What happened?"

"Lawrence took Nicolas away for the weekend. I thought I was going, but it turns out he's teaching me a lesson. Too bad I'm a lousy student."

I put my arms around her. "You're safe now."

"Safe? I'd be safer if I just learned to shut my mouth. This only happens when I provoke him."

"Provoked or not, it's not right."

"I know how it's supposed to work. So, you never told me why you were looking for Lawrence?"

"That friend of mine looked at that crumpled document. He's not sure what it means, but he did say some of the numbers didn't add up. He asked me a couple questions about the guy who sold us the building."

"You bought a building?"

"We did. There were money troubles and we got a deal. It sounds like a few of the tenants were holding back funds. I wanted to ask Lawrence about them."

"I'm not an investor type, but I'm guessing that can't be good."

I let Madeline sign her forms and the nurse gave her a bottle of painkillers. I wasn't sure what to do now. "Should I take you home? Is it safe there?"

"Do you mind if we go to your place?"

I nodded.

"I just need a few hours to regroup."

"Yes." I kissed her cheek. Again those feelings washed over me. She was smiling when I pulled away. "I'm sorry Madeline. I... this... It's wrong. Damn it, you're her sister."

Her eyes danced back and forth, trying to fix on both eyes at once. "It's okay."

"No." I thought about what Heidi had said. "I honestly love Rebecca. I think I want her back so bad that I'm wishing to see her in you. I see her fire, her passion, and her tenderness. I see our memories in your eyes. To me, you might as well be her and that's not fair to either of us, but I can't help it."

She dropped her head down on my chest.

"What do I do, Madeline?" Then, as if under a spell, I said something I couldn't take back. I didn't want to take it back, no matter how stupid it sounded. "Madeline, I'm falling in love with you."

"Don't say that."

"But I am."

"Damn you. We need to get out of here, and we need to talk."

Chapter forty seven

Madeline remained silent while I drove us back to my hotel room. When we got there, Heidi had cleaned up and left. I was wondering how I would explain her. She was a friend who wanted so much more, but I couldn't give it. Madeline was the reason why I couldn't.

She started with a story about a black dress. It made little sense to me until she told me the dress belonged to Rebecca. At that point it made absolutely no sense. Was she telling me she was Rebecca, that this was all a matter of mistaken identity? The answer turned out to be yes. I couldn't speak. This woman in front of me, the one I was so worried about falling in love with, was my Rebecca. She was Rebecca the whole time, yet she was with him, my brother. How could she have done this to me?

"I'm not with Lawrence because I love him."

"But you're with him."

"Not by choice."

"Damn it, you were intimate with him!"

"When I thought I was Madeline, I was trying to wrap my head around all the emotions. He was my husband and that meant for better or worse. As hard as I tried, the sex was never more than a wife's duty. My heart beat for the first time in weeks when I realised who I was. At that point I could only think of you."

"You should have told me."

"I'm telling you now." She tried to continue. "My parents were strangers in the beginning. My brain was cookie dough and

180

because of that, my life became whatever they put into it. They could have added anything, what foods I liked, where I went to school, if I went to school. I wouldn't have known any different. It wasn't until seeing that dress receipt that I figured things out. By then Rebecca was gone and Madeline had taken over."

"You could have left him when you realised."

"I could have, but then Nicolas would grow up without a mother. He'd be raised by a man who treats women like this. In time, he'd become a monster himself. Nicolas was Madeline's son and I owed her."

Her eyes didn't leave mine. They saw the hurt that she was putting me through. I couldn't hide it. She wanted what I had wanted. We deserved each other. I moved in for a kiss. She moved away.

"I can't."

I stood dazed that she didn't want what we had. "I never got over you Rebecca. Your kiss has stirred so many emotions."

"I'm sorry. They've stirred mine too."

I sat down before my legs failed me. How could she have betrayed me like this, continued to betray me? We were in love. We were perfect for each other. Maybe I was wrong the whole time. I had to be. "I think you should leave."

"Do you mean leave Lawrence or..."

I looked over to the door.

"But I don't want to lose you again, Jon. I can't..."

She wanted me and that touched my heart. Sadly she couldn't leave Nicolas. That meant that she'd always be Lawrence's wife. "Think about what you're asking. I'll have to sneak around while you're with him? Let's face it, you won't go anywhere without Nicolas and I can't expect you to. But I can't give you what you want. Besides, I deserve more."

"But..." She reached out and placed her hand on my shoulder. I took it in mine and held it tight. "Johannes, I'm so sorry for putting you through this. I never meant to hurt you and I should have told you sooner. It's not like I've ever done this before."

"You said you thought of me?"

"Once I realised I was Rebecca, I thought of you every day."

That helped, but it wasn't enough. She was telling me she loved me with the same breath that told me she couldn't leave Lawrence. The pain was worse than anything I'd ever felt before.

"I'm really sorry, Johannes."

"Me too." I let go of her hand. "What do we do now?"

She kissed me on the cheek. "Good bye. I'll never get over you and when I get away from this man, and I know I will, I'm going to come looking for you. There's nobody else for me."

With that, she turned and left.

When the door closed I dropped to my knees. I loved Rebecca with every fibre of my being, but that person was gone. When Madeline died, her life took over my Rebecca. She took her over in such a way that she'd never return. Rebecca was indeed gone and Madeline was as alive as she was before the accident. I had to accept this fact and what better way to accept this than a few beers.

I was waiting for room service to bring a second batch of beers when the door opened. Heidi was holding the bottles.

"Ran into room service down the hall. They said these were for you. Are we having a party, Jon?"

I took the beers in one hand, Heidi in the other, and pulled her in for a kiss. I may have been drunk, but I knew she wanted this as much as I did. Her lips were soft and welcoming.

Chapter forty eight

She finished the kiss and looked up at me. "What do I owe the pleasure, Jon?"

"You're beautiful, even with the black eyes, we've always had crazy feelings for each other and you are as real as they come."

She pushed me back. "That's why you thought you were an art thief, cause I'm real."

"Not that kind of real. When you tell me you care for me I know you mean it. I know that if we were to get together you'd want me as much ten years from now as you do today."

"You know I would." She opened two of the beers and handed me one. She knew she had some catching up to do. "Cheers. Now start talking."

"Cheers." I downed the bottle and reached for another. "You hungry?"

"A little. What are you thinking?"

"Dunno. Something we can eat in bed." I pulled the covers back on my side and kicked my shoes off.

Heidi picked up the phone and placed the order. She ordered a bottle of wine, a plate full of strawberries, pineapple and cantaloupe. They were also instructed to bring chocolate and some whipped cream. She hung up and went into the bathroom to freshen up. She didn't come out until room service had dropped off the fruit.

When she came out, I was already in bed with all the food. "You look incredible, Heidi."

She sauntered toward me in just a housecoat. She let it fall open as she made her way around the foot of the bed. I pulled the sheets back for her and stared while she let the robe fall to the floor. Picking up the platter of food she slipped into the bed and nestled in beside me. The platter went across our laps as we sat up and bunched the pillows up behind us.

The sheets covered us from the waist down as we dipped into the food. I had a couple pieces of cantaloupe while she dived into the pineapple. It was fresh and it tasted good. I had to think, and realised that this was the only thing I'd eaten all day. Morning had been busy and the afternoon had killed my appetite, that is, until seeing Heidi lose the housecoat. "This is good."

"Try the pineapple." She put a piece in my mouth and drew her fingers out slowly. She watched me chew it as she grabbed for a spoonful of whipped cream. It slowly made its way toward her mouth.

I was mesmerised. What was she up to?

The spoon was deliberately turned upside down and the dollop of cream landed on her left breast. "Oops."

Like a hungry wolf, I moved in. "Let me get that for you."

I rolled over onto her and let myself grow against her hip while I licked at the cream. She pushed against me and shifted her hips beneath me. Her legs voluntarily moved apart, putting me in position. All I had to do was give my hips a gentle thrust.

I'm not sure why, but I hesitated.

Heidi pushed me off to the side and slid out of position.

"What are you doing, girl. I thought we were…"

"I thought we were, too. What are you really doing, Jon?"

"What do you mean?"

"I had you in the tub naked a couple days ago. You didn't bite. I just invited you in and you didn't jump at the chance. Why? You're not thinking about Madeline, are you?"

"It's not Madeline," I confessed. "She's really Rebecca."

"What?" She scurried over to her side of the bed, almost kicking me in the groin. "Are you kidding me?"

"That's not why I want to…"

"The hell it isn't." She gave me the soft, most caring look I'd ever seen. It was the kind of look a mother might give their newly born child. "Jon, you love that woman. Why would you…"

"She's with Lawrence. She's not going to leave him."

Heidi could see what this was all about. "Because she can't leave that little boy."

"Right, because of Nicolas. It's stupid."

"I am flattered in a weird way that you would want me back now that she's out of the picture, but she's anything but out of the picture. You can't deny the fact that you love her. It's not healthy."

"What's it matter? She doesn't love me."

"She does, but she's been cornered."

"Why doesn't she want to leave him?"

"You can't make her chose between you and Nicolas. That's not fair."

"How is any of this fair for me?"

"Give her time. This is hard on her too." She slipped her naked frame out of the bed and made her way to the bathroom. She returned in her sweat pants and t-shirt. "Now get some clothes on and order me some real food."

"What do you want?"

"How about pasta, and don't cheap out with some pesto sauce. I want a meaty bolognese."

"You got it, and Heidi…"

"Ya?"

"I'm sorry."

"For this? Don't be an idiot." She sat down on the bed beside me and gave me a hug. "You mean more to me than anybody else on the planet. I just want to see you happy. This would have been fun, but if the two of you ever got back together you'd regret what we did. I don't want to be a regret."

"You are one special girl."

"I know." She brought her mouth up to my ear and gave it a nibble. Then in the lightest whisper said, "And if in a year, things don't work out here, come to Germany. We'll finish what we started."

Chapter forty nine

The morning started with another apology, two coffees and a plate of pancakes. Heidi was packed and dressed to leave this crazy city. Order in her world had been restored and she spent the better part of the morning giving Danny instructions.

"I can't wait to get back there. Sounds like my father was in the middle of making some pretty big changes. Now I have to straighten that mess out."

"And you like this job?"

"I'm not just in charge of these men. I also have their families to think about. Although I don't do pensions and benefit packages, they feed their families because of me. And because of me, they don't have to worry about being arrested. I'm not saying that the drug trade is a good business, but the people buying my shit are adults that want to party. They've got the money to spend and want a decent product."

"You're a brave girl."

"Whatever. Can I get a ride to the airport today?"

"Sure."

"And pack up your shit."

"Why?"

"Because you shouldn't be living in a dingy hotel."

"Have you seen my apartment? I kinda made a mess of it."

"Doesn't matter. You're a contractor. It's too hard to work on from here. Besides, you're running away from the real issue. Deal with Rebecca. You know I'm right."

"What if I'm not ready?"

"Too bad." She picked up the phone and asked for the room to be cleaned. She also told them it would be my last day and that I'd be down to settle my bill in an hour. "There. Now you don't have any choice in the matter."

"Thanks, Dear."

"No problem, Darling. I'll even help you clean up."

Room service came as I was zipping up my suitcase. The woman offered to come back, but Heidi told her it was okay to start in the bathroom. The phone rang and I answered it. I listened for a second and then hung up.

"Who was that?"

"Wrong number. When's your flight?"

"Three, but I don't mind getting to the airport a little early. I'll pick up a book. Did you know reading is very therapeutic?"

"Did you read that somewhere?"

"Very funny."

With my suitcase in my left hand I picked up hers with my right. "Ready to go to the airport?"

"You know I am."

I dropped Heidi off at the airport and swung by my apartment. There were three messages from Eddy and two from Marcus. I phoned Marcus first.

"What happened back there?"

"I told you last night. Heidi set up a sting with the Paris police."

"To do what, put her Dad back in prison?"

"It's complicated." There was a lot more to it. There was the police in Germany, the men that had worked alongside her the last ten years and the feelings that weren't meant to be because Rebecca was still alive. Bottom-line, we were free from the Joseph because of her and I was a mess. He wanted to know more about Rebecca and I filled him in as much as I could over a phone. "Want to get together for a beer? It's all pretty crazy."

"I'm going on a road trip up to Rouen. A client wants me to advertise his new lounge. It's some high-tech thing. I'll catch you when I get back. You should phone Eddy though. I've talked to him a couple times now. The guy's okay. He's turned his life around. Did you know he owns a theatre?"

"He's gonna open it soon. We'll have to go."

"He also served as a Stuttgart Scout when he was little. I can't imagine."

We'd heard of the Scouts, a volunteer group headed by the church. Most kids that had anything to do with them were wards of the state or criminals. They were the ones given up on and treated like little slaves.

"Guy had a rough childhood," Marcus added. "Hey, I'll call you when I'm back."

"Sounds good."

Eddy was at the theatre. I helped him move a cabinet upstairs into the projector room in trade for a beer at the pub down the street. I chose a stout wheat beer. The barmaid that brought it also brought a bowl of peanuts—breakfast.

"So how did you sleep last night?" I asked.

"What sleep? I kept waiting for the damn police to kick down my door. Did you know any of this was fake when we entered that museum?"

"I had no idea. When she didn't care that you two split, I knew something was up. I didn't even know when we were handcuffed and thrown in the back of one of the cars. That was when she told me the painting was…" I remembered my promise not to say anything about it being a fake. "…was worth millions."

"That thing? It was ugly."

"It wasn't ugly. I kinda liked it. Damn thing was a Van Gogh."

"That was a Vincent Van Gogh? I never saw a signature."

"That's because he never signed it."

"Is that why Joseph wanted it?"

"Partly that, partly because he saw it and fell in love with it in prison." I took a drink from my beer. "Last night, Heidi told me about the painting. Her father liked it because it looked like a typical Paris café. He always had a love for the city."

"That, and it was worth millions."

"What he didn't know was that it was Van Gogh's modern version of Da Vinci's Last Supper. There is a central figure surrounded by twelve individuals. He looks like a waiter, but it's Jesus. A cross shines directly behind him on the wall and the black figure leaving on the left is supposed to represent Judas. I think it was a fitting choice for a man about to go back to prison for a very long time."

"You know he'll be even angrier when he gets out," Eddy surmised.

"He'll be so old he'll forget why he was put there." I was hopeful.

"True enough."

"Hey, Marcus told me you were a Stuttgart Scout."

"I don't talk about it. It was nothing." Eddy downed his beer and put the glass down. "He shouldn't have told you that."

"It's okay. I was just wondering…"

"I said I don't want to talk about it."

Chapter fifty

A couple of days after driving Heidi to the airport, my apartment was beginning to take shape. I'd pushed her and Rebecca out of my thoughts and started to focus on me. It had been a while since I'd done that. Our company was in good hands and this place needed walls patched, paint and trim. I'd just spent the day putting the first coat of paint on the walls. The phone rang while I was digging through the fridge for anything that might resemble supper.

"Hello?"

"It's Heidi. How are you doing?"

"I'm painting. How's it going on your end?"

"Good. It's like I never left. Are you sitting down?"

"Do I need to?"

"Grab a seat because what I'm about to tell you is pretty big." She waited while I found a spot on the couch. "That company that you bought with your brother has, or is, filing bankruptcy."

"How can he do that? I'm a fifty-fifty partner."

"I don't know. My business doesn't do bankruptcy or even file any kind of paperwork. I'm no help to you. I think you need to talk to Lawrence."

"I will."

"Just be careful, Jon."

I'm not sure what I was thinking but I put on a clean shirt. Was I worried about what Madeline, I mean Rebecca, might think of me? I didn't put the lid on the paint or clean up the tray and brushes. I thought about it on the drive over. I'd be buying new brushes.

I wanted to pull into the driveway but it was full. The street was full. I ended up parking two blocks away and that was good. I needed to calm down before I got there. I didn't. I paced the sidewalk in front of the driveway for a couple of minutes.

This was my brother. He had no reason to screw me over. Heidi must have been given bad information. Why would he do this? This was just as much his money as it was mine.

Since I couldn't calm down, I decided to go in. I walked past the two cars in the driveway and up to the front door. I reached for the doorbell and stopped. Would he answer the door or would she? Him, I could handle. Him, I'd ask the question, hold my ground until I got the truth.

What if Rebecca answered the door? Was she in on this? Had she been thinking about me? Did it matter?

I slowly took in a deep breath. I exhaled slowly and knocked. There was no answer, yet I could hear voices. I knocked again, harder.

Rebecca opened the door. She was dressed in Madeline's clothes, happily playing the part of her dead sister. It was pathetic and I had to look away. In the dining room, the guests were seated around the table. Like in the painting, it also looked like the Last Supper.

"Lawrence, what the hell did you do to our company?"

"Yes," Lawrence replied. "By all means, come in. We were only sitting down to have a meal."

Ingrid got up from her chair. "Johannes, *sie du müsst wirklich gehen*."

"No. I'm not leaving until I get answers. My apologies to everyone else, but this is important." I looked back at Rebecca and she looked scared.

She grabbed my arm and pulled me back toward the front door. "We need to talk, come."

"Not now." I pulled my arm free. "I just heard rumours that you filed bankruptcy for our company today, that this great deal of yours has gone bad."

Ingrid got up. "Trust me, Johannes, this is not the time."

191

Lawrence made a mental note. "Look, I'll also lose money, so let's get back to the subject at hand. Were you invited tonight?"

I looked around and to Rebecca. She wasn't wearing the bandages and the make-up couldn't hide Lawrence's wrath. "No."

"Then maybe we should talk tomorrow. Come by my office, say around nine."

"Why would you do this? We were partners." I stepped into the room and past Ingrid. There was no leaving without answers. "We're brothers."

Lawrence cleared his throat. "It's business."

"What happened to our company? I thought you said we got a good deal on it."

Ingrid interceded, "Can we talk, tomorrow?"

Shaking his head in disgust, Lawrence looked over to his friend, Captain Frank Delacrois. The look was meant to get him off his paid ass and do something. Frank remained seated.

He turned back to Ingrid. "And what business is it of yours? If you like, you can join us tomorrow at nine. I'll give you both a rundown on the particulars."

"You know what? This works too." Ingrid dropped her hands to her lap. "I did a little digging for my friend, Johannes. Seems it was never a good deal. There were tenants holding back rent. Michael tried to get the money through litigation, but these tenants had connections. This caused quite a few cash flow problems. Any idea who these tenants were?"

"This conversation is over." Lawrence tried to remain composed, "It's the middle of dinner and I don't think this is appropriate table talk."

"I don't care." I took another daring step forward. I wasn't about to back down, not after losing all that money. "I'd like to know who they were."

Lawrence wasn't about to back down either. "Get out of my house."

Chapter fifty one

Ingrid continued, "It was the offices of Daniel Debois and Lawrence Trembley. Their firm owed close to two year's rent on eighteen offices. It's one hell of a cash flow problem and Michael couldn't evict them due to a loophole."

"I think you should leave with him." Lawrence chuffed.

"You did this, Lawrence?" I could feel the blood draining from my face. "You had this planned from the start, didn't you?"

Lawrence said nothing.

My only comfort was that Rebecca looked as shocked as the rest of us. "What did you do, Lawrence?" she asked.

"I simply unloaded some debt."

"Let me see if I got this right." Anger was bringing the blood back to my face. "You crippled our building by forgiving the debt that you owed, and then you declared bankruptcy? How could you?"

"That can't happen with a bankruptcy," Ingrid's father piped up. "Moves like that would be illegal without your consent. Shareholders, even the ones that aren't fifty-fifty partners need to be informed in writing before transactions like these can take place. You knew that, didn't you Mr. Trembley?"

"Of course. I know how a bankruptcy works." Lawrence sharpened his glare. "There's no proof that I didn't tell him. He likely lost the note. And I think you should mind your own damn business."

I started for Lawrence, and Ingrid's father stepped in my way. Chairs slid on the hardwood as everyone except for Lawrence got to their feet.

"Lawrence, was this a bankruptcy?" Rebecca asked. As his wife, Madeline, she'd be implicated. "Or is the building for sale?"

"Not any more," Lawrence offered.

"That's right. Someone's already bought it," Ingrid offered. She looked around and shrugged. "What? I do my homework."

Rebecca looked over to her. "What are you saying?"

"Cam Bolen bought it," Ingrid announced. "I found out yesterday, Madeline."

"There we have it. It wasn't a bankruptcy. I bought it, I sold it." Lawrence leaned back in his chair, giving her the chance to concede. "I've done nothing wrong. Cam Bolen bought my building. He got one hell of a good deal too. And when did losing my shirt become a crime?"

"Cam Bolen?" Rebecca asked. "Why did you tell me it was a bankruptcy?"

Lawrence lit a cigar and the glow matched the fire in his eyes. "Because as always, you weren't listening. I found a last-minute investor, nothing illegal, and nothing shady. My brother and I made an investment that went south quick. It even surprised me to find a buyer so quickly, but I've never been one to look a gift horse in the mouth. We didn't get much, but at least we have something. We'll settle tomorrow, Jon. I'll write you a cheque."

I found myself morbidly intrigued. "What kind of cheque are we talking?"

"I'd rather talk about it tomorrow."

"And I'd rather know today."

"Okay. After legal fees and my commission, it'll be a little over eighteen thousand Francs."

I could feel my legs weaken. "That's not even a fraction of what I gave you. My parents worked hard for that money. But this isn't even about the money. We were sharing our parent's legacy. How could you do this?"

"He can't." Ingrid answered.

"You're still here?" Lawrence took another puff. "It was my company. I think I can."

"Oh, you can sell it. It's Cam Bolen. He can't buy it."

Her father was the first to raise an eyebrow. "Do you know Mr. Bolen?"

"That would be difficult. Monsieur Bolen does not exist." Then she added, "He was our final guest."

My confusion continued.

Rebecca asked, "If he doesn't exist, then how can he be here?"

"I spent the day calling in quite a few favours," Ingrid answered. "They were all leading nowhere. The man was a phantom. He didn't exist. I mean he did, but nobody knew him. I was taking a break, a glass of wine on a patio, when it hit me. You see I used to do anagrams when I was a kid. Dad got me started on them to bolster my I.Q. I'm not sure if it worked, but it sure helped me find this Cam fellow."

"Anagrams?"

"Yes, Madeline. You take a word like 'tar' and turn it into 'art' or 'rat'—the same letters, different words. I was looking at Cam Bolen and playing around with the letters. Then I remembered Johannes telling me about his long-lost brother. This Mac Noble Agency fostered him. Imagine my surprise when I scrambled the letters of Cam Bolen into Mac Noble. It tossed a few red flags in the air. Then I found out that this agency also helped kids find jobs."

"Weren't you one of those kids?" I asked. It felt weird hearing Ingrid call her Madeline. She obviously didn't know. Did Lawrence?

"He was." Ingrid announced. "And when he left the agency, he got a most fortunate job at the Department of —."

Lawrence cut her off as he got to his feet. His chair teetered on its back legs as it slid back. "You little bitch, who do you think you are? You enter my house, eat my food, and run your damn mouth on things you know nothing about. You need to leave, now!"

"But..." She looked over to Rebecca. "I was invited."

"Where was this job?" I asked.

"The Department of Records," Ingrid answered.

195

"Who the fuck are you, anyway?" Lawrence put his hands up as if to mock a surrender. "You know what, it doesn't matter. Dinner's ruined. Get the hell out of here." He turned to Captain Frank Delacroix. The man remained seated. "All of you, get out!"

Monsieur Latteur positioned himself between Ingrid and Lawrence.

Ingrid's father also moved closer to her. "I think we need to settle down."

Lawrence turned to Rebecca. "What do you think you're pulling, inviting these people into our house? You have three seconds to get them out of here."

She just stood there. "I, uh…"

Ingrid's father stepped forward. "Don't blame her. I know you don't deal directly with me, but your firm deals with my bank." He pulled his wallet out and placed a business card on the table. "We've already started a full investigation on this venture." He slid the card toward Lawrence. "I'll be expecting your full co-operation."

Lawrence picked it up and started to read. As he did, his face paled. He looked up at them and opened his mouth to say something. Nothing came out. The shocked look caused his partner, Daniel, to grab the card. His face also drained to a ghostly grey.

Scarlett looked around the table and then back to Lawrence. "What's going on? This isn't a party. Who are these people? Who's Madeline?"

"I'm his wife. And how exactly do you know Lawrence?"

Her words were timid. "Why, I'm his girl—"

Lawrence slammed his fist on the table. "Don't answer her you idiot."

"Yes Scarlett, best not to upset the man." Ingrid reached past her father and slowly lifted the last vacant plate, revealing an enlarged photocopy of a passport picture with the name Cam Bolen under it. It was the one that looked a lot like a young Lawrence. There was also a snapshot of Lawrence kissing Scarlett in front of a hotel. "I think upsetting him is my job."

"That's it, Frank." Lawrence grabbed his friend by the shoulder and shoved him toward her. "I want these people out of my house." He turned to Alain Beauchene. "I'll see you on

Monday. As for now, you can take your wife and your stupid kid and get out."

Police Captain, Frank Delacroix remained frozen as he stood there. "I'm sorry, Lawrence. I can't help you with this."

"I mean it Frank, you owe me."

Mr. Latteur stepped forward, pulling out his badge and a folded sheet of paper from his jacket pocket. It was a search warrant. "Frank, I advise you to take this man into custody."

Frank spoke softly as he slowly reached for his cuffs. "Yes Commissioner."

Lawrence lunged against the table as he fired his glass at Rebecca. "You bitch. You think you're going to get away with this? After all I've done for you."

Ingrid snapped. "Done for her. Look at her face."

Commissioner Latteur held up the passport picture of Lawrence, a.k.a. Cam Bolen. "Do you know this man, Lawrence Trembley?"

Lawrence kept his stare on his Madeline as he wrestled himself free from his friend. "You're going down with me, bitch. This wife of mine is a fraud. I found out yesterday that she's not who she says she is. Did you know she killed her sister? Now she's been pretending to be my wife."

Frank followed him. "Where are you going Lawrence?"

"To get the proof."

He paused at the entrance of his study for effect. "This woman isn't my Madeline. She's Rebecca. And if that's not enough, she's been seeing my brother behind my back."

Ingrid held up a copy of Lawrence's birth certificate and tore it in half. "This is fake. You're no more Johannes's brother than you are mine."

I watched as she tore it up. He wasn't?

Chapter fifty two

Lawrence stopped at the door to the study. "For weeks they've been preying on my feelings. Scarlett was all a part of it. She's a plant. They've been holding me captive in this marriage, planning to ruin me if I didn't go along with them. She wants the house and my son."

I grabbed the two pieces of the certificate. "This is a fake?"

"I'm sorry, Johannes," Ingrid answered as she put a hand on my shoulder. She knew how badly I wanted this. "He's not your brother. He's an opportunist. This was all made up."

"I can't believe you're all buying their bullshit. It's all a scam." He turned to Rebecca. "You're good, but I have proof."

"It's true," Dr Pierre Needham weighed in. "He recently brought it to my attention. There's a taped confession."

"Go get it, Monsieur Trembley." Commissioner Latteur signalled Frank to keep an eye on him.

I looked over to Rebecca and she was staring at me. She was terrified.

Lawrence returned with a tape recorder and a tape. He pushed the play button and cranked the volume. At first there was only silence. Then the machine clicked off.

Lawrence swore and fumbled the tape over, pressing the play button again. And again, we waited. It was quiet for a second before starting with a song.

"What the hell?" He forwarded the tape and pushed play one last time.

The song played for close to a minute before Ingrid broke our silence. "You like the band Meatloaf. Uh, what's your point? You still hungry?"

The tape recorder sailed across the room. It caught Rebecca off guard and struck her in the shoulder.

"Tell them who you are, you conniving whore." Lawrence slipped past Frank and shoved her to the floor. Frank quickly pinned him against the wall.

Ingrid ran over to her. "Shit. Are you okay?" Her eyes and one of her hands dropped down to her belly. If no one had noticed before, they had now.

It was the way she held Rebecca's stomach. It forced me to see the bump. "What, are you pregnant?"

She didn't answer. The fear in her eyes was all the proof any of us needed.

"Let go of me Frank, I'm not going anywhere." Lawrence pulled himself free again and headed for the bar. "I think a drink is in order."

I locked eyes with Rebecca. Not only had she cheated on me with this asshole, but she was pregnant with this man's child.

Lawrence looked back at us as he opened the cabinet. "Does anybody want to join me in a drink?"

I never saw the gun. Lawrence levelled it at Rebecca's head and the puff of smoke was immediate. The shot whistled past her and struck the hardwood frame of the china cabinet.

A second shot came my way. It also missed shattering something in the kitchen. This asshole had lost it and Rebecca, not my favourite person at the moment, was pregnant. I needed to keep her safe so I inched toward her.

"Stop right there brother or the next one won't miss."

Then Lawrence quickly turned the gun toward Commissioner Latteur. He already had a hand inside his jacket.

"Before you get any crazy ideas, you and Frank need to pull your guns out and drop them on the floor."

Frank dropped his gun to the floor first, followed by Commissioner Latteur. He put his hands up to shoulder height and took a step toward Lawrence. "You do realise, this is a mistake? You don't have to escalate this. Right now, there are a few fraud charges. I'll tell you how the courts work. You'd be out in less than five years. Shoot one of us and it becomes life."

"I'm out in five." Lawrence shrugged. "Doesn't sound bad, except what am I out to? I've lost my child, my house and my reputation." He trained the gun back in my direction. "This woman says she's my wife. That's a lie."

I started to inch toward Rebecca again. "You don't need to do this."

Lawrence readied a third shot and snarled, "Stay away from her."

He trained the barrel of the gun back to Rebecca. The first two shots had damaged furniture. They were warning shots. This one wouldn't miss her.

"Lawrence please," she pleaded.

"Please what? You've won. You get my house and my child." He started toward her, firming his grip. "Thanks to you, I'll be looking at a life sentence."

She tried to correct him. "Commissioner Latteur said five years."

The gun was quickly pointed in my direction. Another puff of smoke left the barrel. The accompanying wet thud of a bullet hitting flesh dizzied me. The burning sensation in my chest dropped me to my knees.

"Jon!"

I heard her yell as I fell to the floor, felt her hand on my chest. Suddenly I wanted to tell her I loved her and that nothing mattered but her. I couldn't. My lungs were tightening around the burning in my chest.

"There we go. I think we can all agree that it's more than five years." Lawrence moved closer to us while he trained the gun on the others. "If you don't want this to get any worse, then you'll do as I say."

"Just don't kill him," Rebecca begged.

Through squinted eyes I could see him grab her arm and jerk her to her feet. "Why not, my dear? Do you love him? Would you miss him? Things might go a whole lot better if you just admit it."

"You're crazy."

"Whatever. Admit you love him and I won't put another slug in his chest."

"Why are you doing this?" she cried.

"So that's a no." He raised an eyebrow. "Suit yourself."

I let my eyes close. I had wanted to hear her say it too.

"I beg you, Lawrence. Don't! I'll say whatever you want me to say."

He stood there holding the gun on me while his mind spun. "Change of plans." He grabbed a handful of Rebecca's hair and dragged her toward the door. "We need to go."

"I'm not going anywhere with you."

I opened my eyes to see him dragging her across the hardwood floor. It was like a bad dream. Was I dreaming? I let my eyes close again as she disappeared from sight.

"No, Jon." It was Ingrid's voice. "Stay with us."

But I was fading fast. Footsteps raced past me as the frantic voices called for an ambulance, police, and …

I could hear Ingrid crying, but it was like she was a million miles away. Someone was holding me. A light rain was landing on my face, but I was inside.

The burning in my chest had faded. Everything had faded. I was ready.

"Don't leave us, Jon," a voice whispered.

Again I tried to speak but couldn't. I felt a kiss on my temple. Another raindrop landed on my brow. It had to be from Ingrid.

I'd miss her.

Chapter fifty three

Feather-light sheets pinned me to the bed like blankets made of steel. My eyes were open, yet I could barely see. This was a hospital bed. That was my guess because I was sitting slightly upright. I blinked a few times to clear away the sleep before carefully rolling my head to the left. There was Ingrid. She was staring across the room at something outside the window.

I took a minute to build up the strength to speak. "Whacha look'n at?"

"Oh my God. You're awake." She immediately gave me a smothering hug. She recoiled when I winced in pain. "You scared the shit out of me."

"You thought I was dying?"

"No. You're German and far too stubborn for that." She laughed while a tear dribbled down her cheek. "How are you feeling?"

"Weak, sore." I tried to pull myself up a bit. Memories from what had happened were starting to untangle themselves from the snarled mess. One in particular stood out. "How's Rebecca doing? Is she really pregnant?"

Ingrid just stared.

"She's pregnant, isn't she?"

"She is," Ingrid admitted. "I feel bad for the way you found out."

"It is what it is. So where is she?"

"She was kidnapped. Lawrence has her."

"Where did he take her?"

"Again, we have no idea. I'm worried for her."

"Why? He won't hurt her. She has his child inside her."

"No, Jon. That's your child."

"It...uh, seriously?" A wave of disbelief washed over me. This was fantastic and yet terrible. If Lawrence knew it wasn't his, he'd kill her for sure. "What are the police doing?"

"They're doing what they can, which isn't enough." She took my hand. "And you need to worry about getting better right now. That bullet nicked your abdominal aorta. It wasn't a bad nick, but you lost a lot of blood. You'll need to rest up."

"You knew an awful lot about Lawrence. Why were you looking into him?"

"Rebecca wanted me to do that. She was so scared this asshole would screw you over and she was right. The police will be able to recover most of your money because of her."

"She said she couldn't leave him."

"She loves that nephew of hers. He's a cute kid."

"I know, but..."

"She loved you very much, Jon. Thing is, you didn't need her like Nicolas needed her. She really didn't have a choice. It had nothing to do with you."

I didn't want to hear that. I needed to stay angry with her. "Do you think she's okay?"

"I don't know."

"You know she came to my hotel room. This was after Lawrence hit her with the snow globe and I took her to the hospital. She confessed that she was Rebecca and I threw her out."

"Don't, Jon. You were hurt."

"All I could think about was him on top of her."

"That was a nightmare. She never enjoyed him."

She let go of my hand and walked over to the foot of the bed. My food tray was wheeled down there and flowers had been heaped onto it. It felt good to see them.

"You have quite a few friends," she said while she snooped through them. One of the cards was plucked from a beautiful bouquet of red roses. "Who's Heidi?"

"Why? Are those from her?"

She gave me a sideways glance. "I bought you carnations. Eddy got you a nice garden mix, and that was only after I twisted his arm. This Heidi has expensive tastes."

"She's a good friend."

She put the card back. "If you say so."

I wanted to tell her about the art heist, the police and how she reacted to me after she found out Rebecca was still alive. She was right to say no. I would have regretted it and regretted her. Knowing how much she wanted to be with me, only a true friend would have said no to me.

"I say so."

"The boy's awake?" Eddy asked as he entered the room. "It's about time."

"Hey, Movie Man," Ingrid joked. "Good to see you."

"You guys have met," I asked.

Ingrid answered. "We're best of friends now."

"Yeah. Nothing like sharing a dozen coffees while you wait for your friend to come out of surgery." Eddy handed her a coffee that he'd picked up from downstairs. It was why he'd left. "Sorry, Jon. Not sure if you're ready for one yet. I can get you a water."

"I'm good."

Eddy continued, "So I heard you were looking for some long lost brother."

"I thought I found him too. He had a birth certificate and everything."

"Ingrid did some checking, says the guy has a scar from a broken leg or something. Did you see the guy's leg?"

"No. I thought the birth certificate would suffice."

"I could have told you the guy was a fake. I wish you would have said something."

"How would you have been able to tell the guy was a fake?"

"How long have you known me, Jon?"

I couldn't really say. It was as long as I'd known Heidi or Marcus. "Since middle school?"

"We've known each other since I was six. You were four. Your Mom used to visit me at the park."

I had to think for a second. Then it hit me. "Oh my God. You're…"

"Teddy."

"That's right. I forgot about that. We used to play together as kids. That Nun used to bring you by the swings. We'd play for a couple hours and then you'd be taken away. I used to call you Teddy."

"You couldn't say Eddy, yet Teddy was easy." He shook his head.

"How often did we see each other?"

"About once every couple weeks. Eventually I was adopted and I moved away. We didn't see each other again until middle school. I was two feet taller and became your Fast Eddy Cruiser."

I turned to Ingrid. "The guy was a rocket on a bicycle."

He'd brought me down memory lane and I was enjoying the ride when the pieces all fell into play. "Oh shit! I called you Teddy, because I couldn't say Eddy. Eddy was Edgar, wasn't it?"

"I've always preferred the American version of the name."

"That's right. You were always dazzled by the Hollywood folks."

"Not a lot of celebrities called Edgar in Hollywood," he admitted.

"Lots of them are called Eddy, though."

"And you couldn't even get that right," he laughed, "So Teddy it was."

"Lift up your pant leg."

"Finally." Ingrid triumphantly put her hands up. "I didn't think you'd ever clue in."

He lifted his pant leg up to reveal one whopper of a scar. "You found me, Bro."

"You knew this the whole time?" I stared as if the man had just appeared out of thin air. "Why didn't you tell me?"

"I wasn't sure how you'd take it. Your Father never would have allowed me in your life. Could you imagine Christmas dinner? That being said, our mother couldn't imagine us not knowing each other, even if it were only as friends. She made sure we got to know each other, even if it were only two strange little kids playing at the park. When all that Joseph crap happened, we all went in different directions. My family moved me to a different city and we drifted apart. I kept tabs on you and our mother from a distance. That's how I found out about the accident."

I tried to take it all in. "Wow. So you're my Edgar."

"I am."

I held my arms out. "It's great to see you again."

He carefully hugged me back. "I agree."

Chapter fifty four

I was getting used to my hospital routine. In the morning I'd have two eggs, toast and watery coffee with Ingrid and Marcus. In the afternoon I had vegetable soup, crackers, and several doctors running tests. They wanted to see how my blood pressure reacted to exercise. For supper I had meatloaf, which I loved, potatoes and peas. Shortly after that, Eddy would pop by and we'd go over those early visits. He'd tell me what he remembered about me and our mother. It was a simple ritual, yet it worked.

If only one of them could have given me some kind of news on Rebecca. That was the topic they all seemed to be skirting. There was a good chance she was okay and trying to find a way to get free. There was also the chance that she'd be found half-buried with leaves by some hiker. There was a third and much worse option. That was that we never find her and never know. Would he be torturing her years from now? I couldn't think about it.

"Good afternoon, Jon."

I'd expected one of two doctors, or one of four nurses. It was Heidi and she had two police officers and a bag with her. "Hi." I straightened up as I worked the button that controlled the bed. It slowly lifted me.

She set the bag down in the chair beside my bed. "I'd like you to meet Lieutenant Bisset and Commissioner Latteur."

"I remember Mr Latteur. He was there when…"

Heidi cut me off. "When you were shot and Lawrence kidnapped Madeline."

I had almost slipped up and said Rebecca. Ingrid had explained the plan to have Lawrence arrested. She also explained how they had covered Rebecca's tracks so she couldn't be implicated. It had worked fine until Lawrence pulled out the gun. I held out my arms for a hug. "It really is great to see you."

She gently hugged me and kissed my cheek. "I just can't stay away."

"Do we have any news on Madeline?"

Commissioner Latteur answered. "I'm sorry. We haven't found her yet. We do have some news on your investment. We've confiscated Mr. Trembley's assets. They're in the process of making things right. It may take a while, but Michael Antoine will buy his building back and the balance of Lawrence's assets will settle his debt from unpaid rent."

"And when you find him?"

"They'll be arrested. Lawrence's crimes will put him away for a very long time."

"Isn't Madeline innocent?"

"She's his wife. There is no innocence in these matters." He dropped his head knowing that it wasn't what I wanted to hear. She wasn't the one signing the documents, but she must have known something. She could have done something about it? The man was a tyrant. "There's something else."

"What do you mean?"

"It happened this morning," Commissioner Latteur admitted.

Heidi moved in closer and took my hand for strength. That frightened me.

"What's going on here?"

"Madeline's child was placed in the custody of Lawrence's parents. About three hours ago the child went missing. We think Lawrence took the child."

"Did he take him for Madeline?" I asked. Heidi squeezed my hand. It wasn't a reassuring squeeze. It was more of a you-don't-want-to-hear-the-answer squeeze.

"We don't even know if it was Lawrence. When we questioned the parents, they knew nothing and they were hiding something. It was like they were lying for somebody. We're sending pictures of him out to all the major cities in France. He won't be able to stay out of the city forever."

"Do you have any questions for me?" I asked. "I'll tell you everything I know."

"We don't have any further questions. We know he lied about being your brother and that you barely knew them."

"I'd met them a few times, had dinner with them once."

"Any idea where he might have taken her?" Commissioner Latteur asked.

I shook my head. "No idea."

"We just stopped by to let you know you should see all the money you invested, less legal and administrative fees."

"That's great. Thank you."

They left me alone with Heidi. I couldn't help but think she'd used her influence to help me get my money back. "Thanks. I know you had something to do with that."

"My kids deserve to eat pancakes and real syrup, not dry bread and water." She laughed. "Now I need you to do me a favour."

"Anything. I owe you that much."

"Do you trust me?"

"Of course."

"They're thinking of releasing you today. Do you feel healthy enough to travel?"

"I'm getting rather bored with the place. What do you have in mind?"

"Don't open this until I'm gone." She pulled out a slip of paper and handed it to me. "I need you to go see this person. You'll need to call first to get an address. That's all I can tell you."

"Do they know who took Nicolas?"

"There's a very good chance, but you can't involve the police."

"Why do I need to see this person? I think I should call the police." I corrected myself. "Actually, you should have called the police."

"Hence the trust, Jon. No police."

I held up the paper as if to open it and was stopped. "How did you get this?"

She shook her head. "Some might say it's luck, me being in the right place at the right time."

"Is that what you say?"

"I say, you make your own luck." She got up, leaned over and kissed me. "I sincerely doubt we'll ever be rid of each other so I'll stop saying goodbye. I really came to see for myself that you were okay."

With that she left. It was true that we'd never be rid of each other. Good friends were stuck with each other for life.

I yelled out to her. "Don't forget to take the kids. I'm tired of feeding them."

"Great." Her laughter echoed back to me from the hallway. "Now I have bus money."

Chapter fifty five

The piece of paper was torn on two edges, like it was needed last minute and ripped from something handy. I opened it to see a name. It was Anastasie. There was no last name, just a number. The area code was not a Paris one. When the doctor entered the room I quickly folded it up and tucked in under the sheets.

"Are you feeling good enough to go home, Johannes?"

"I'm feeling fine. Tired, but fine."

"We've got you on a couple pain meds that zap the strength. You should only have to take them a couple more days."

"I'm not in a lot of pain."

"Maybe we can change them. We've got a different painkiller that's not that strong and you can function while you're on them. I'll send a few with you and you take them as needed."

He checked my blood pressure and scribbled something on my chart. "Okay. You are officially released. I'll need you to come back in a week for further testing. Take care of yourself, Johannes."

He held out his hand and I shook it. "Thank you, Doctor."

My clothes were folded in the drawer of the nightstand by my bed. I got up and pulled them out. The pants had been cut off me and the shirt was bloodstained. Then I spotted the bag that Heidi had brought. It was sitting on the chair and had designer jeans, a new shirt, underwear and socks in it. There was even a bottle of what used to be her favourite cologne. I had received a bottle of the stuff when I was eighteen. She claimed she couldn't keep her hands off me when I wore it. She'd thought of everything.

I quickly dressed, let the nurse know I was ready for my wheelchair ride and let her wheel me out of the hospital. Outside, I got on the Metro and made my way to my car. Yellow police tape was draped across the front of Lawrence's house like Christmas garland.

Back home I went straight to the phone. I dialled the number and waited.

"*Bonjour*?" the woman asked.

"Hello?" I answered.

There was silence for a second. "I trust you got my number from Heidi?" Her accent was a heavy French one.

"Who is this?"

"My name is Ana. Have you contacted the police?"

"I was told not to." There was a pause so I added, "Heidi is a good friend of mine. If she tells me not to contact the police, I listen."

"This is good. I have information about Madeline."

"You mean Rebecca."

There was another short pause. "It seems that maybe one is the same."

"It is a little confusing. What do you know?"

"I know that a child was picked up at…"

"You mean kidnapped."

"I mean relocated."

"Does Lawrence have him? Is Rebecca okay? If you know where he is, you need to call the police. The man is dangerous."

"First, we need to talk."

"We are talking. Is Rebecca okay?"

"I need to know I can trust you. I'll answer all your questions, but you cannot involve the police."

"You can trust me. Where are you?"

"Taped to the underside of a bench is a note. It's the bench closest to where you first met Rebecca. Go there and make sure you are not followed. There'll be an address. I hope to see you in a few hours."

"And you'll tell me everything?"

"Everything and more. Be quick, but be careful. Come alone."

I dropped the phone in its cradle and hurried down to my car. The place she was talking about was Ile de la Cité. It was a little park on the west side of the island. It was also where I had stepped on Rebecca's sandwich the day we'd met.

I started north and watched the rear view mirrors more than the road. After a few turns, three back alleys, and a busy traffic circle, I made my way to the park. Parking as close to the bridge as I could, I went down a flight of cement stairs and quickly made my way to the elm tree.

There was a bench close to where we had sat and I took my place on it. Letting my hand casually run along the underside of the bench, I found two pieces of gum and the note. I read it. The woman was in Val de Reuil.

I stopped by the theatre on the way out of town. Eddy was there.

"Look who's back from the dead."

"Feels good to be out."

"Did you see Heidi?" he asked. "She's in town again. I'm guessing she wanted to see that you were okay."

"She stopped by the hospital. I think she's really gone this time."

"I'll bet she's a busy woman now that her father is back in prison."

"She is. Police stopped by too. Said they'll have my money for me. That Michael guy will get his building back and Lawrence will pay him what he owes from his estate."

"Have they found the man?"

"Not yet. They've confiscated his assets."

"And Madeline? Any word on her." He added, "Ingrid kind of filled me in on a few things."

"No." I wanted to tell him what I was up to. I should have said something, but didn't. Instead I offered the man a deal. "Is there any chance I could invest in your theatre?"

"Like a brotherly thing? I'd have thought the last brother would have scared you off a venture like that."

"He wasn't my brother. What do you say?"

"I'd really like that. Do you know how to run a popcorn machine?"

We laughed and sealed the deal with a brotherly handshake.

"I think I can learn."

I left Eddy to hang a light fixture while I stopped back at the apartment. There was something I needed before heading out.

Chapter fifty six

The drive on the A13 was a fast one. The highways were a lot clearer once you got out of the city. Much like the autobahn, there wasn't a strict speed limit as long as you were driving respectfully. The weather had also cleared up as I headed west. What was once dull and overcast, had broken into cottony clouds scattered across a blue sky.

The Val de Reuil exit came up and I made my way to a traffic circle. From there I finished the drive to a smaller pastel yellow house with a roof steep enough to accommodate an upstairs. Unlike most of the homes here, this house stood alone on a modest yard. There was ample street parking.

I stepped through the gate, walked up the sidewalk and knocked on the door. My heart was fluttering like a moth under a streetlight. I had no idea what I was walking into and trust was everything. I hope Heidi knew what she was talking about. Oddly I didn't feel fear. It was more a curiosity.

The door opened and my heart stopped. It was Rebecca who answered and she looked like she'd been beaten up. It took me a minute to speak. "Are you okay?"

"I'm good." She took me in and I sat on a chair across from her in the kitchen.

"So that was you on the phone? You had quite the accent."

"I couldn't say anything over the phone. I'm sorry about that."

"I can't believe it's really you." I couldn't pull my eyes off of her. She had a black eye and the bandages. "What happened, Rebecca?"

"My name's Ana. You need to start calling me that, especially out in public."

"What?"

"I'm Anastasie Colombre Léone." She showed me a passport. "My husband, Benoit, and I were in a tragic car accident a week ago. He died. It's just me and my son now."

"You mean Nicolas."

He was sleeping in the other room. The house was half the size of the one in Paris, but it seemed cosy. I counted two bedrooms, a bathroom, and a large back yard.

She slid a second passport toward me. "He's Théo now. It's a name game we're playing for right now, but if the game goes on long enough, he'll forget he's Nicolas."

"Why are you doing this?"

"After the car accident, I remembered everything. This time I had a say in what happened next. I decided to choose this life for my future. Rebecca had already died, and Madeline, she'd spend the rest of her days in court if they ever found her. Lawrence had so many shady dealings and my sister knew about all of them. She was okay with them."

"Really?"

"She helped him pick this place. There's no paper trail. That makes her an accomplice. If I go back to being Madeline, it makes me an accomplice. If they can prove I knew anything, I'll rot in jail. I don't think I deserve that, nor does Nicolas, I mean Théo. The boy needs a mother."

"You could be Rebecca again."

"Rebecca was just as guilty. She should have left him when she realised who she was. There'd be motive for all that crap he said at the house. They might even believe his death was murder. There'd be an investigation. You'd be implicated. So would Ingrid. Whether I was Madeline or Rebecca, I'd have to come up with answers that I just don't have."

She was right. Either way she'd be a wanted felon. And then there was her missing nephew. "Did you kidnap Nicolas?"

"No. I had his grandmother's consent. She knew what her son was, what her husband is. She also knew what her grandson would become if he stayed."

She and I talked, we cried, and eventually we both agreed that Théo would be better off with me. I promised that I'd call her whenever I was in Paris. We would do a quiet lunch, so she could stay in touch. Her husband could never know. The woman would become his Auntie Catherine.

"And your parents?"

"I've filled them in as well. They know everything. I'm not saying they're happy about it, but they're starting to get used to me being the one that flies left of centre. They'll be coming over for dinner in the next few days. I'll always find ways to keep them in my life, although it won't be easy."

I sat there absorbing, processing, and trying to understand where I fit in. She poured me a cup of coffee. I wanted to ask how Lawrence had died. There were all kinds of questions that should have been asked. I couldn't.

"This isn't ideal," Rebecca continued, "but for the first time I'm the one in control, albeit living the life of Ana. Regardless, I'm happy. I have Nicolas, my memories as Rebecca, freedom from a torturing husband, and no lawyers trying to have me thrown into the deepest dungeons of France."

"So who's Ana?"

"More like what's Ana's. It's just a name. Think of me as a second version of Rebecca, or a third. I'm the one without the baggage, the guilt or the past."

"No past?"

"I'll always have the memories, like the day with the ducks and that flattened baguette."

I took her hand and placed a gentle kiss on the back of it. "I've missed you."

"You can't imagine how I've missed you." She trained her eyes on mine and it melted my heart. "I've hurt you so much." She put a hand on my chest.

"You mentioned a car accident." I looked down at her stomach. "Is the baby okay?"

"Your baby is doing very well." Her eyes instantly welled.

I let my arms envelope her and she dropped her forehead on my chest.

"What do we do now?" she asked.

I let go of her and stepped back. I turned away. "This is the hardest thing I've ever had to do, but it's something I must do."

I turned around to face her again. My face was sober, German sober. I was looking for Rebecca, but that woman was gone. Madeline was also gone. She was Ana now.

I took a step toward her and dropped to one knee. Then I took her hand and, not having a proper ring, gave her knuckles a gentle kiss. "Ana, would you..."

"Yes!"

I stood up, dug into my pocket and pulled out a ring that I'd wanted to give her weeks ago. It had two birthstones on it, hers and mine. I slipped it on her finger and it fit like I knew it would.

"Are we..."

I shrugged. "I don't know how we do this, or what we'll be doing, but I do know I want to be doing it with you."

She hugged me like she used to when we were first dating. Even though she was now Anastasie Colombre Léone, Rebecca Harrows was the woman on the inside. Her memories, compassion, and love for me was as real as it had always been.

I looked around at the house while she held me. "It's nice."

"And it's paid for. Do you think you could bring a few of your things here? I have an awfully big closet. I'm sure I could find room for a couple of shirts and a pair of pants."

"I have an awfully big closet as well. If I put a few of your outfits in mine, there might be more room in this one. I could bring more things." I added, "I have shoes."

"That's a good idea." She smiled and it warmed me like a fireplace in the winter. "I have one other question."

"Anything. Ask away."

"Who is this Heidi woman?"

Chapter fifty seven

Chilliwack – December 24, 2015

I watched my wife, Ana, stand at the window while day turned to night. She is easily as beautiful as the day we met. Outside, winter continued to drift down from the sky. For the last eight hours the snow had turned our driveway into an impassable sea of white. The trees in our yard, and we had many in our yard, looked full again as they carried the weight of a millions tiny little snowflakes. Thankfully, everyone had arrived hours ago.

Across the room from me the fireplace roared and it caused me to look up at the cards on the mantle. One, in particular, caught my eye. Much like the fireplace, that card also warmed my heart.

The little smiles of our family were gathering around the tree. The supper had been delicious, but it was time to open gifts. I parked myself on the far side of the living room by the Christmas tree. It was time to go to work. The responsibility of handing out presents was a job I loved. With a bellyful of rum and eggnog, I was up for the task.

I pulled my red Santa hat on and started handing presents to Théo and his wife, Annette. Our daughter, we called her Rebecca, got several gifts, as did her husband Pierre. The smiling little girl with chocolate on her chin was our Madeline. She was Rebecca's daughter and our granddaughter. She'd recently turned four, but there were days when I swore she was smart enough to be in her teens.

Ana and I were married a year after the accident. We figured it was a respectful amount of time for our friends and families. I adopted Théo and Rebecca, who was secretly my daughter. After five years in Val de Reuil, we decided to vacation in Chilliwack. I loved it so much, we moved that year. I could see in my wife's eyes, how badly she missed her home.

It had frog ponds, mountains and acres of open fields for Théo to roam around in. There were sunsets that took your breath away. Canada was peaceful, the kind of place I could get used to.

We soon sold the house and the strip-mall to buy a farm a few miles from where Ana grew up. We also rescued a golden retriever from the dog pound. A second house sprouted onto the property the following year and her parents quickly moved into it.

Ingrid and Marcus eventually got married and had a daughter. Sienna was three years younger than our daughter Rebecca, who was born five months after that fateful dinner party. We have all remained the best of friends and once a year we manage to meet up somewhere. Last year they came and stayed at our farm. We took them to the pond and Ana walked Ingrid through the first decade of her life. The kids rode the legs off the neighbour's ponies.

I kept my apartment in Paris and make the occasional trek out there. Eddy and I are business partners now and I need to keep abreast on my investment. Well, that and I love a good movie when there's popcorn involved. He still beats me at crib.

Once again I looked up at that card on the mantle. The Christmas card was a Van Gogh and it came from Stuttgart. I get one every year. Ana has never minded my getting the cards from Heidi. She understands the bond we share is strong, almost as strong as the one her and I share. Besides, she loves the unique cards. The one from last year had Santa eating pancakes with twelve elves around a large table. She had signed it Heidi plus one.

I meet up with her on occasion when I go to Paris. Sometimes I even take her to Eddy's theatre for a movie. She's the new Heidi now so she never tries anything. The woman only wanted me to be happy and she understands that I am.

Johannes

We don't talk about the fact that she's seeing somebody when we get together. The girl has always loved her privacy. She's happy and that's all that matters.

I just hope that if they have children, she doesn't sell them for bus money.

Other Books by Kevin Weisbeck

Madeline's Secret

Madeline suffers from amnesia when she wakes from the car accident that killed her sister. Her parents, husband, and small child are all strangers. As she accepts these people into her new life, she uncovers a secret, one so dangerous that it could ruin her if it ever got out.

The Darkness Within

A victim of his own bad choices, Johnny Pettinger is stranded following a plane crash in a remote mountain wilderness. His injuries are serious, but they're not the only factors preventing him from getting home. In order to do that, Johnny needs to shine a light on the very reason for his being there, the ***Darkness Within***.

The Divine Ledger

Detective Violet Stormm is a woman on a mission. She'll do anything to catch the man responsible for a series of gruesome murders. Victor Wainsworth is the man doing the killing. He's fuelled by a ledger, a book that not only holds the names of his next victims, but clues to the ***Eve of Humanity***.

(This is the first of five books in the ***Eve of Humanity*** Series)
(This book also introduces the ***Violet Stormm*** Detective Series)

About the Author

Kevin Weisbeck is a Canadian author, born in Kelowna, British Columbia and currently living in Okotoks, Alberta. He's had several short stories published in magazines and newspapers, and currently has one in McGraw-Hill's iLit Academic Program.

He can usually be found on the couch with his laptop in front of him and his Ragdoll cat, Franklin, on his shoulder. It's not an ideal writing set up, but Franklin doesn't mind. Otherwise Kevin enjoys hiking, kayaking, camping, photography and golf (when the weeds and water don't get in the way).

Made in the USA
Middletown, DE
18 May 2019